Giambatista Viko; ou,
Le viol du discours africain

GEORGES NGAL

Giambatista Viko; ou, Le viol du discours africain

Edited by

David Damrosch

The Modern Language Association of America

New York 2022

85 Broad Street, Suite 500, New York, New York 10004-2434
www.mla.org

To order MLA publications, visit mla.org/books. For wholesale and international orders, see mla.org/Bookstore-Orders.

The MLA office is located on the island known as Mannahatta (Manhattan) in Lenapehoking, the homeland of the Lenape people. The MLA pays respect to the original stewards of this land and to the diverse and vibrant Native communities that continue to thrive in New York City.

Cover illustration: *Faces VI*, by Angu Walters, ArtCameroon.com.

Texts and Translations 39
ISSN 1079-252x

Library of Congress Cataloging-in-Publication Data

Names: Ngal, M. a M. (Mbwil a Mpaang), 1933- author. | Damrosch, David, editor.
Title: Giambatista Viko : ou, Le viol du discours africain / Georges Ngal ; edited by David Damrosch. Other titles: Viol du discours africain
Description: New York : The Modern Language Association of America, 2022.
Series: Texts and translations, 1079-252X ; 39 | Includes bibliographical references.
Identifiers: LCCN 2021050672 (print) | LCCN 2021050673 (ebook) | ISBN 9781603295819 (paperback) | ISBN 9781603295826 (EPUB)
Subjects: LCGFT: Novels. Classification: LCC PQ3989.2.N462 G5 2022 (print) | LCC PQ3989.2.N462 (ebook) | DDC 808.83--dc23/eng/20211202
LC record available at https://lccn.loc.gov/2021050672
LC ebook record available at https://lccn.loc.gov/2021050673

Contents

Introduction

Published in 1975 on the cusp of our global era, *Giambatista Viko; ou, Le viol du discours africain* is an exceptionally timely work today—and a delight to read. Georges Ngal's self-obsessed antihero is an African intellectual eager to make a name for himself on the world stage. Professor at an unnamed university, Viko belongs to an institute of African studies that is riven between Europe-centered cosmopolitans and xenophobic Africanists who reject Western culture out of hand. He has been struggling for two years to write the great African novel, a work that he longs to finish so that he can be invited to conferences in Paris and Rome. Yet instead of writing he spends his time on the phone with his disciple and sidekick, Niaiseux, scheming against his Africanist colleagues, developing a cutting-edge theory of writing, and looking for ways to pad his résumé.

Viko knows that he has to produce a major work if he is to achieve his goal of becoming "le Napoléon des lettres africaines," but he is aware that blending African and European cultures is no simple matter, even as he believes that Africa can no longer be held apart from Europe. For all his vanity and self-promotion, Viko is a shrewd observer of the scene around him; he sees "africanolâtrie," for example, as a subtler form of westernization. Casting about for inspiration, he recalls the *Scienza nuova* (*New Science*) of his namesake, the Italian humanist Giambattista Vico, whose 1725 treatise asserts that all language began in the poetic cries of primitive people. Inspired, Viko decides that he can plunder African oral traditions to create the revolutionary novel that will be his ticket to international fame. (Appropriately, although "Giambattista Vico" and "Giambatista Viko" are spelled differently, they sound almost the same when spoken.) Viko reaches the point of writing, using an extravagantly experimental style: "tantôt des brusques opacités, tantôt des profondes transparences. . . . La ponctuation? N'en dis rien." His goal is within his grasp; but then disaster strikes. The Africanists gain the upper hand at his institute, and they go public with a series of accusations against him: of having his articles ghostwritten; of outright plagiarism; of sexual indiscretions with an Italian associate, a devotee of free love and French erotica; and above all, of betraying Africa by plotting to prostitute the mysteries of oral culture for Western exploitation—in the novel's subtitle in French, *viol* can mean either rape or a legal violation, and the term also suggests the theft, *vol*, of African discourse. Outraged, a group of tribal leaders arrest Viko and Niaiseux and stage a show trial, which concludes with devastating—but ultimately rejuvenating—results for our hero and his friend.

An extraordinary satire of problems of identity in a globalizing world, *Giambatista Viko* is a pathbreaking exploration of the vexed relations between European metropolitan centers and peripheral former colonies. Ngal's own life has spanned the globe, with periods spent living and teaching in Africa, Europe, and North America. He was born in 1933 in what was then the Belgian Congo, and he came of age during the country's struggle for independence. Bilingual in French and in one of the Bantu languages, he studied Latin and Greek in Jesuit schools and then in a seminary, where he joined the Jesuit order. In a 1975 interview, "Authenticité et littérature" (G. Ngal, *Œuvre* 2: 197–210), he said that his teachers "se caractérisent par esprit libéral et humaniste. Ce qui développait chez leurs élèves la contestation, l'esprit critique et anticonformiste. Chose extraordinaire sous le ciel colonial" (2: 197).

Ngal went on to study philosophy and theology at Lovanium University in the capital, Kinshasa, graduating in 1960, the year that saw the establishment of the independent Democratic Republic of the Congo. He spent two years teaching Latin and Greek in a Jesuit secondary school, then went to Switzerland to pursue graduate studies in literature. After earning a doctorate at Fribourg in 1968, where he wrote his thesis on the Caribbean poet Aimé Césaire, he returned to his homeland as a professor of francophone literature at Lovanium University. He soon became the first Congolese to head the department, which was formerly run by expatriates from France. His life took an unexpected turn in 1971, when he fell in love. He left the Jesuit order and married, though he remained a lifelong Catholic, and his novels make frequent references to the Bible. He moved to the Faculty of Letters at the University of Lubumbashi, in the southeast of the country, where one of his colleagues was the novelist and critic Valentin-Yves Mudimbe. Mudimbe had also studied abroad, receiving a PhD in philosophy in Belgium before returning home to teach and write; he and Ngal developed a rivalrous friendship. Ngal then spent two years abroad, from 1973 to 1975, first as a visiting professor at Middlebury College and then under the auspices of a foundation that sent him to teach francophone literatures in two-week stints at a series of universities in Canada, Belgium, and France. He began with residencies at the Université de Québec and then at the Université de Sherbrooke in southern Quebec.

It was in Canada that Ngal determined to become a novelist as well as a scholar. As he wrote in a late essay, "Impact migratoire sur l'écriture" (G. Ngal, *Œuvre* 1: 83–92), during his stay in Quebec City,

> Un après-midi, je descendis dans la vieille ville où une brocante avait lieu. Je tombai par hasard sur un vieux livre d'un auteur français. Le hasard voulut que j'ouvris la page suivante: "Pauvres écrivains africains!!! Quand ils se mettent à écrire, c'est toujours pour nous rabattre une seule idée: ce que leurs ancêtres leur ont légué à travers les mythes, les legends, les contes, etc." Ce reproche ne me quitta plus et s'installa en moi pour toujours.
>
> Quelques jours après, je me trouvai à Sherbrooke. Installé dans un hôtel, au premier étage. Toujours habité par l'idée reçue à la brocante de Québec. Je décidai sur le champ de répondre à cet écrivain. La premier phrase de ce qui deviendra *Giambatista Viko ou le viol du discours africain* fut écrite dans cette chambre. La rencontre ici fut dominée par un mot: écrire. Un petit mot tout bête, quelques lettres seulement, pour traduire un labyrinth de pensées ou de rêves, de mystères. . . . (1: 84)

He began working on his novel during the balance of his teaching tour, then completed it upon his return to Lubumbashi.

Once back at his university, he received a chilly reception from Mudimbe and other colleagues who regarded him as building his career abroad instead of attending to problems at home. As Ngal worked on his novel, the character of Viko took on various traits of Mudimbe, both in appearance and in his love of surrounding himself with disciples. Even so, Ngal probably expected his friend to be a sympathetic reader, as Mudimbe had published a well-regarded novel two years before, *Entre les eaux*, on comparable themes of cultural alienation. Mudimbe's hero, Pierre Landu, is a priest who has studied in Europe but then abandons the priesthood after his return to the Congo, where he enlists in a Marxist guerilla band. Landu never finds himself at home, however, as he is always caught between the shifting currents of cultures and of ideologies. Yet Mudimbe didn't appreciate Ngal's more satiric treatment of an alienated intellectual. Instead, he took the book personally, and he actually lodged a legal complaint against Ngal, accusing him of defamation. Remarkably, then, Ngal found himself—like his own protagonist—subject to legal action by his academic rival. This could be called a situation of life imitating art, though now Mudimbe was accusing Ngal's art of all-too-closely mirroring life. In an angry essay for a weekly newspaper, he claimed that Ngal's portrayal of Viko was a thinly disguised attack on himself and several colleagues, in terms that were "précises, publiques, méchantes." He writes that "il ne s'agit pas de fiction pure mais d'interprétation mensongère des faits réels et d'attaques intentionelles, surnoises et malveillantes," and he concludes: "Il est dommage que le professeur NGAL ait besoin, pour créer une œuvre, de piller et de falsifier la vie ou les comportements de ses collègues" ("L'affaire *Giambatista Viko*" [*Zaïre-Hebdomadaire*]).

The case was dismissed, but relations with his colleagues grew so tense that Ngal soon moved to a university back in Kinshasa. Even four decades later, in an essay collection published in Ngal's honor in 2014, the editor included an appendix that reprinted Mudimbe's attack ("L'affaire *Giambatista Viko*" [Cibalabala]) together with a defense of the novel in the same newspaper—which was unsigned but probably written by Ngal himself ("L'affaire 'Giambatista Viko'"). More than that, the appendix includes photocopies of letters proving that Ngal hadn't been expelled from the priesthood back in 1971, as his enemies had claimed, but had received permission from his bishop and from Rome to return to secular life in order to marry (Cibalabala 262–67). Old disputes die hard.

In the same year that he published his novel, Ngal also published, in Senegal, his illuminating study *Aimé Césaire, un homme à la recherche d'une patrie*. He went on to publish extensively on Congolese and other African writers, and he was appointed a professor of francophone literature at the Sorbonne in 1980. He taught there and elsewhere in Europe until 1991, when he returned to Kinshasa to serve on a national educational commission. He was later elected to the Congolese parliament, and worked for many years with UNESCO and other international organizations before eventually retiring to France.

Quite apart from individual rivalries, the conflictual academic situation in the seventies reflected the tumultuous politics of the country as a whole. Following decolonization in 1960, the leaders of the newly independent Democratic Republic of the Congo were divided between westernizers and nationalists who wished to emphasize African cultural identity. Such conflicts could be found in many former colonies, but the Congo's colonial history had been particularly fraught. In the mid-1870s, having failed to persuade his parliament to establish a formal colony in central Africa, King Leopold II of Belgium set up a private corporation, loosely modeled on the British East India Company, which had become a de facto colonial power in India a century before. He treated the Congo thereafter as his personal possession. In 1885 his Congo Free State achieved international recognition, aided by the promotional work of the journalist-explorer Henry Morton Stanley. Renowned for having located the supposedly lost explorer-missionary David Livingstone deep in the forests of Tanzania, Stanley went on to dramatize his African adventures in bestsellers such as *Through the Dark Continent* and *In Darkest Africa*. He served for a decade as King Leopold's principal agent in creating trading stations along the Congo River and establishing relations with tribal chieftains. He detailed his success as colonial empire builder in *The Congo and the Founding of Its Free State: A Story of Work and Exploration*, which is filled with praise of "the munificent and Royal Founder of the Association Internationale du Congo" (386).[1] In 1899, Joseph Conrad drew on Stanley's works, as well as his own experience as a steamboat captain on the Congo River, for his novel *Heart of Darkness*.

Growing international outrage at the violence and naked exploitation in the colony forced Belgium to assume formal control in 1908 with the establishment of the Belgian Congo, though foreign commercial interests continued to play a major role in the colony. What had been de facto slavery in the Congo Free State was gradually replaced by wage labor, and an increasing number of people moved into urban centers, where there developed a Europeanized middle class, whose members were known in the patronizing term of the day as *évolué* Congolese. A growing number of them began to receive university educations abroad, or in the Congo itself after several universities were founded in the 1950s.

Economic development went along with simmering political conflict, and an increasingly radical independence movement achieved the Congo's independence from Belgium in 1960. The new Congolese government was formed through an uneasy alliance of leftists and liberals, with the Marxist prime minster Patrice Lumumba governing together with the pro-American Joseph Kasavubu, who served as president of the republic. This government rapidly fell apart, and a civil war ensued, fueled by separatist movements in two of the country's richest provinces. The involvement of private militias hired by Western mining companies made the situation worse, as did Cold War maneuvering by the United States and the Soviet Union, each of which sought to use the conflict to advance its own interests in the region.

Lumumba was assassinated by opponents supported by Belgium and the CIA, and several chaotic years ensued. Finally, in 1965, power was seized by the army's chief of staff, Joseph-Désiré Mobutu, who established a dictatorial regime. He held power for over thirty years, murdering many opponents and potential rivals, all the while enriching himself and his cronies on foreign aid and through the expropriation of domestic industry. Mobutu cultivated close relations with Charles de Gaulle, Richard Nixon, and Romania's dictator Nicolae Ceauşescu (and later with Valéry Giscard d'Estaing, Jimmy Carter, Ronald Reagan, and George H. W. Bush), while also playing on nationalist sentiments. He renamed his country Zaire and promoted *zaïrianisation*, requiring his citizens to abandon the European names they had often been given at birth and to adopt African names instead. He dropped his own name of Joseph-Désiré and took the name of a warrior great-uncle, becoming Mobutu Sese Seko Nkuku wa za Banga (All-Conquering Warrior, Who Goes from Triumph to Triumph). As a result of this policy, during the 1970s Ngal ceased to write using his baptismal name, Georges, and chose instead the symbolic name Mbwil a Mpang (Spiritual Leader from Mpang).

It was under this name that Ngal published *Giambatista Viko* and a sequel, *L'errance*, which largely takes the form of dialogues between Viko and Niaiseux. Their conversations are interspersed with appearances by Pipi de la Mirandole, whose name wryly recalls the great Italian humanist Giovanni Pico della Mirandola, famous for his *De hominis dignitate* (*Oration on the Dignity of Man*). Viko and Niaiseux debate questions of identity and the role of the intellectual in society, as they rediscover the riches of African village life and as Viko works toward a fuller integration of his European and African selves—the possibility of which is still very much an open question in *Giambatista Viko*. As a now wiser Niaiseux says at the conclusion of the sequel, they have achieved a multidimensional and polymorphous mode of communication. "Nous parlons en effet plusieurs langues, témoins, dans ses paroles originelles, ses mots, ses tournures de phrases, ces eaux profondes et différentielles qui constituent la diversité de l'humanité dans ses divers visages" (M. Ngal, *L'errance* 141). This linguistic diversity goes along with a diversity of genre. In both books, as Ngal later wrote in "Impact migratoire sur l'écriture," he had no interest in writing plot-driven realistic novels: "C'eut été s'enfermer dans la suprématie d'un genre; s'enfermer alors dans la tradition française et occidentale" (G. Ngal, *Œuvre* 1: 85). His novels blend very different modes, including dream visions, essayistic discussions, extended quotations, and poetic reveries.

By the time Ngal wrote *Giambatista Viko*, Mobutu's repressive kleptocracy was in full flower, and open dissent was impossible. Yet Ngal and other like-minded writers fiercely maintained their independence. As Ngal wrote in a retrospective survey, "Littérature zaïroise, cette méconnue" (G. Ngal, *Œuvre* 1: 31–39), the literature of the period "n'a rien avoir avec la politique culturelle bidon du jour. Chacque auteur suit son inspiration, en toute indépendance. C'est là peut-être le plus significatif de la littérature zaïroise. Elle ne sacrifie ni au goût ni à l'idéologie du jour." At the same time, "S'il faut lui chercher un dénominateur commun, il convient de reconnaître que c'est d'abord une littérature d'exilés de l'intérieur et de l'extérieur. . . . Un exil vécu comme une prise de conscience d'un déchirement culturel, d'une exclusion ou d'une séparation spatiale" (1: 35). Mudimbe's *Entre les eaux* is one of the works that Ngal cites together with his own novel as examples of the literature of internal exile.

Giambatista Viko says nothing about national politics, but the show trial it depicts, and the tribal elders' brutal methods of punishment, clearly echo the regime's practices. Yet Ngal's trenchant satire extends to his own protagonist, hilariously dissecting Viko's vanity, self-promotion, and unstable mixture of insecurity and megalomania. In the novel's opening pages, Viko fawns over a visiting European intellectual, Sirbu, whose Romanian name casts an ironic glance at Mobutu's friendship with Ceauşescu.[2] Throughout the book, Viko compares himself to a pantheon of great French writers, while at the same time he obsesses over critical comments on the poverty of African culture by Jean-François Revel, who may be the unnamed writer whose condescending account of poor African writers had inspired Ngal to begin his novel in Quebec. Most notably, in his 1970 bestseller *Ni Marx ni Jésus*, Revel had argued that revolutionary social change could be expected only from the United States and not from a stagnant Europe or an underdeveloped Third World. It would have been no comfort to the Francophile Viko that Revel had no more hope for progress from France than from Africa.

Ironically as he is presented, Viko is a surprisingly sympathetic character, embodying real tensions experienced by people with a foot in two different cultures. This situation has been acutely felt by many Congolese writers, participants at once in a multilayered African culture and a global francophone intellectual life; the Congo is, in fact, the largest French-speaking country in the world apart from France. If Viko bears a certain resemblance to Mudimbe, he is equally a portrait of his own author. Conversely, a description Mudimbe gave in an interview of his hero Landu could apply both to himself and to Ngal: "Il est africain, et viscéralement africain. Mais en même temps, il est occidentalisé, qu'il le veuille ou non. Ce qui fait de lui ce qu'il est, comme intellectuel, réside, justement, dans la complémentarité de ce double caractère: d'être, à la fois, africain et occidentalisé" (qtd. in Semujanca 23).

Giambatista Viko can be read at once as a Congolese novel, a francophone novel, and a contribution to world literature. Ngal had an encyclopedic knowledge of African literature both in French and in English, and his novel reflects his search for an alternative to what he saw as the dominant modes of folklorism and social realism in much of African fiction. In the broader context of francophone *littérature-monde*, he has Viko quote North African intellectuals such as the Algerian poet Rachid Boudjedra, as well as the *Cahier d'un retour au pays natal*, by Ngal's favorite Caribbean author and longtime friend Césaire. In the background are Léopold Sédar Senghor's poetry and Chinua Achebe's 1958 *Things Fall Apart*, as well as Cheikh Hamidou Kane's *L'aventure ambiguë*, Ousmane Sembène's *Xala*, and other novels of the 1960s and early 1970s. Yet Viko, who looks down on his fellow Black Africans, never quotes them, and he doesn't realize that he is a far less exceptional figure than he supposes.

Giambatista Viko was part of a wave of African novels of the 1960s and 1970s written out of disenchantment with the results of decolonization. Where earlier works such as *Things Fall Apart* had probed the evils of colonialism, usually in a realistic mode, a range of African writers began to critique the authoritarianism and corruption of many postcolonial

African regimes: for instance, Ahmadou Kourouma in *Les soleils des indépendances*, written in exile from his native Côte d'Ivoire, and Sony Labou Tansi in *La vie et demie*, written in a mode of magical realism, in which a dictator's victim refuses to accept his death and keeps reappearing in the story. Another notable example is Mali's Yambo Ouologuem, whose prizewinning historical novel *Le devoir de la violence* sharply critiqued the long involvement of Mali's rulers in the slave trade. Ouologuem's novel has further relevance because its author, like Viko, was accused of plagiarism; some passages of *Le devoir de la violence* were taken from novels by Graham Greene and by the French writer André Schwarz-Bart. Stung by the controversy, Ouologuem retreated from writing, after publishing two further books the next year: a set of essays on the politics of race and gender, *Lettre à la France nègre*, and an erotic novel, *Les mille et une bibles du sexe*—perhaps providing an inspiration for Viko's Italian girlfriend and ghostwriter Castino Paqua, who treats the French erotic novel *Emmanuelle* as her bible of free love.

Ngal extends to language Ouologuem's critique of political and sexual violence. His alternative title for *Giambatista Viko, Le viol du discours africain*, builds on a common trope of the European violation or rape of colonized cultures. This theme is found, for instance, in Wole Soyinka's 1975 play *Death and the King's Horseman*, and more starkly in the play's precursor, Duro Ladipo's *Oba Waja (The King Is Dead)*, whose powerless hero Elesin declares that "My charms were rendered impotent / by the European" (81). As Maëline Le Lay has observed, in the 1960s and 1970s a number of African writers were seeking to reverse the European conquest; she quotes the Algerian writer Kateb Yacine's statement that "la langue française appartient à celui qui la viole et non à celui qui la caresse" (85). At the end of *Giambatista Viko*,

Niaiseux becomes a direct victim of the warring masculinities around him.

Seduced by French culture, Viko constantly measures himself against French models: not only classic writers such as Honoré de Balzac, Gustave Flaubert, and Marcel Proust, but also the surrealists, in whom Ngal became deeply interested while working on his study of Césaire. Viko quotes André Breton and the poets Robert Desnos and Michel Leiris, and he cites examples of the surrealism-inspired ethnography that sought to rejuvenate French culture through the study of traditional native societies. Atop the bookcase in his study sits a bust of the decadent poet Isidore Ducasse, self-styled Comte de Lautréamont, whom the surrealists had adopted as a precursor; the presence of the bust is appropriate, in view of the accusations leveled against Viko, since Lautréamont asserted that poetry is based on plagiarism.[3]

Further, the novel draws extensively on contemporary Parisian thought. Viko is a disciple of the Marxist philosopher Louis Althusser, and Niaiseux cites the psychoanalytic theories of Jacques Lacan. Viko's search for a dazzling new mode of writing owes a good deal to the theories of *écriture* (writing) developed in Paris in works such as Roland Barthes's *Le degré zero de l'écriture* and Jacques Derrida's *L'écriture et la différence*. Ngal's novel can be read more generally as an academic satire, in the vein of David Lodge's *Changing Places* and *Small World*, both of which similarly hinge on rivalries between self-promoting literary and cultural theorists. But unlike Lodge, Ngal is seriously engaged in the theoretical debates he stages in his novel, and his tale has affinities with a tradition of philosophical fictions dating back to eighteenth-century works such as Denis Diderot's *Jacques le fatalist et son maître* or, a century later, Oscar Wilde's dialogues "The Decay of Lying" (*Artist* 290–319) and "The Critic as Artist" (341–407). Behind all these works stand Plato's dramatized dialogues.

As we read *Giambatista Viko*, we're constantly challenged to find our way amid the book's shifting currents of dialogue, reflections, dream visions, and sometimes brutal action. The primary focus of Ngal's novel is the contradictory yet complementary interplay between African orality and literacy derived from European culture. Ironically, Viko obsesses about recovering a lost orality while talking constantly on the telephone, sometimes to two people at once, a receiver at each ear. He doesn't even understand the Bantu language of the elders who put him on trial, and their speeches have to be translated for him by young up-and-coming technocrats. When Viko is accused of choosing "l'univers du livre—l'espace scriptural" in order to carry out his "tentative de désacralisation de l'oralité," he wonders whether the elders are really thinking in these terms or whether the translator is showing off his sophistication by embroidering their harangues; the elders' speeches come to Viko, and to us, thoroughly imbued with the Western discourse they reject. We also have to consider how far Ngal's own book embodies Viko's ideal for a new kind of *écriture*, and whether his novel does create the synthesis of African and European cultures that Viko apparently can't achieve but that his nativist accusers may not be able to escape.

Giambatista Viko is a creative contribution to the language debates also seen in English in the dispute between Chinua Achebe and Ngũgĩ wa Thiong'o on the merits and disadvantages of writing in English versus an indigenous language. Viko's search for an orally infused French can be compared to Achebe's rejection in the 1960s of the literary viability of local languages (such as Ngũgĩ's Gikuyu) and assertion of the need to write in the colonizers' language:

> Let us give the devil his due: colonialism in Africa disrupted many things, but . . . on the whole it did bring together many peoples that had hitherto gone their several ways. And it gave them a language with which to talk to one another. If it failed to give them a song, it at least gave them a tongue, for sighing. There are not many countries in Africa today where you could abolish the language of the erstwhile colonial powers and still retain the facility for mutual communication. Therefore those African writers who have chosen to write in English or French are not unpatriotic smart alecks with an eye on the main chance—outside their own countries. They are by-products of the same process that made the new nation-states of Africa. ("African Writer" 58)

Achebe asserts that "for me there is no other choice. I have been given this language and I intend to use it" (62), even as he emphasizes that African writers need to remake English and French for their own purposes. Less high-minded than Achebe, Viko does indeed have an eye on the main chance, and yet he also embodies his creator's fascination with indigenous oral styles and performative modes of storytelling (a theme further developed in *L'errance*, which includes tales that Ngal's wife had recorded in Congolese villages). For Ngal, oral tradition involves individual creativity as much as tribal collectivities. As he wrote in a 1977 essay in the American journal *New Literary History*, "Beneath stereotyped formulas jealously retained by the conservatism and conformism of each generation, there occurs a true labor of creativity that is not the work of an anonymous community or of associations due to pure chance but is rather the product of the active dynamism of the individual genius" (M. Ngal, "Literary Creation" 336). Ngal's hero seeks to make his way between independence and authoritarianism, conformism and creativity, French culture and proverbial lore.

Giambatista Viko is also a work in dialogue with world literature. At the time he decided to write it, Ngal had been voraciously reading world literature in French translation and in English. Viko quotes Johann Wolfgang von Goethe and Robert Musil and cites his namesake Vico's *Scienza nuova* by its Italian title, and he prides himself on his ability to drop English and Latin phrases into his conversation along with his many French references. When Viko and Niaiseux are thrown into prison, Niaiseux cheerfully anticipates serving as Plato to Viko's Socrates, hoping to record for posterity the final thoughts of his condemned master. In "Impact migratoire sur l'écriture," Ngal recalls that as he was working on the novel he drew on his experiences in Switzerland, Germany, and England as well as in Canada and France. His travels had included three months in England, where "la langue de Shakespeare résonnait en moi avec des accents particuliers. Une phonologie étrange! Séjours non extérieurs à mon écriture!" (G. Ngal, *Œuvre* 1: 85).

Though Ngal's frames of reference were primarily African and Western, he was already well aware in 1975 of a broader global world. Viko hopes to achieve worldwide fame, and having his work appear in the right languages is an important part of his plans. As he tells Niaiseux,

> Aucun savant aujourd'hui ne peut se passer de la connaissance de plusieurs langues internationales. Connaître l'anglais—je ne parle pas du français, la chose va de soi—l'espagnol, le russe, c'est bien. Le japonais, c'est encore mieux; le chinois c'est encore dix fois mieux car l'avenir, la clé de l'avenir, appartient à l'Asie, plus particulièrement à la Chine. Les Occidentaux ont terriblement peur du péril jaun.

> Mais combien de temps peuvent-ils pétendre tenir le coup. Ils savent lutter contre la fièvre jaune, la juguler. Mais contre la péril jaune, ils ne peuvent rien.
>
> Des traductions ! Ça allongera la liste de mes publications.

Not that Viko knows Chinese or Japanese himself; he plans to ask his visiting colleagues Sing-chiang Chu and Hitachi Huyafusia-yama to translate some of his articles. He wants to get the essays published with the translators' names suppressed, so as to give the impression that he has done his own translations. Marxist that he is, Viko has a passing qualm about the ethics of exploiting his colleagues' labor in this way, but Niaiseux reassures him that "[d]éontologiquement parlant," it isn't intellectual dishonesty at all, but simple collegiality.

Ngal's double-edged satire extends to the racially freighted discourse in which Viko participates even as he resists it. In the passage just quoted, Viko mocks the Westerners who fear what they describe as the "Yellow Peril" without understanding that China is rapidly becoming the political and economic equal of the West, soon to be its superior. That Viko's institute hosts Asian and Eastern European scholars situates it within the broad outlines of the Non-Aligned Movement founded in Belgrade in 1961 as an alliance of postcolonial and peripheral countries against the Cold War hegemony of the United States and the Soviet Union. Yet even as he asserts the equality of African and Western cultures, Viko allows that "d'habitude, j'ai un mépris du Nègre," and he gives Niaiseux credit for being only three-quarters Black, calling him "un métis"—using the racist term apparently in a positive sense. As Clarisse Dehont has observed of Ngal's portrayal of Viko,

> le fait que les propos racistes sont proférés par un Noir amène dans un premier temps de l'humour dans le récit, puisque le racisme est poussé à l'extrême par un personnage lui-même victime de propos stéréotypés et racistes au sujet de sa couleur de peau. Pourtant, l'objectif poursuivi, comme dans toute satire, n'est pas tant de faire rire le lecteur que de pousser celui-ci à une réflexion sur l'intériorisation par les Africains des stéréotypes les concernant. (166–67)

Ngal's eminently worldly novel is a compelling meditation on the perils of identity and artistic creation in a world of unequal power relations, where vanity, self-defensiveness, and a will to power pervade every group. As such, *Giambatista Viko* gave no comfort to any side in the debates on decolonization and postcolonialism of the seventies and eighties, and it poses a continuing challenge to the optimistic notion that ideas and identities readily flow across cultures in today's global village. To date, it has received little attention beyond studies of Congolese literature, but with the Modern Language Association's two-volume edition, in French and in English, and with a Chinese version to be published as well, Ngal's self-promoting, self-reflective hero is finally achieving the global presence he always felt his genius deserved. *Giambatista Viko* is a novel whose time has come.

Notes

1. This phrase appears in a chapter focused on the difficulties of dealing with native middlemen in the ivory trade that was central to the economic exploitation of the Belgian colony. Stanley's chief conflicts are with a chieftain named Ngalyama, a landless slaveowner who "had nothing but his unfounded pretentions, his unreal claims, his loud bully's voice, and his insatiable appetite for the dues of blackmail" (Stanley, *Congo* 387). Ngal could have taken some of Viko's traits from Stanley's portrayal of the aptly named Ngalyama.

2. The philosopher and novelist Ion D. Sîrbu was imprisoned as a dissident from 1957 to 1963 by the Ceauşescu regime, a fact that may add to the suspicion surrounding Viko's dealings with foreigners. Sîrbu was little known internationally, unlike A-list figures such as Jean-Paul Sartre; Viko takes whoever he can get.

3. On Césaire's surrealism, see Michel 59–94. On the surrealists' championing of Lautréamont, see Ungureanu 88–111. Accusations of plagiarism have periodically been leveled against minority or non-Western writers who have appropriated elements from canonical works; see Miller.

Works Cited

Achebe, Chinua. "The African Writer and the English Language." *Morning Yet on Creation Day: Essays*, Anchor Press, 1975, pp. 55–62.

———. *Things Fall Apart*. 1958. Anchor Press, 1994.

"L'affaire 'Giambatista Viko.'" Cibalabala, p. 260.

Arsan, Emmanuelle. *Emmanuelle*. Éditions Fixot, 1988.

Barthes, Roland. *Le degré zero de l'écriture*. Éditions du Seuil, 1970.

Césaire, Aimé. *Cahier d'un retour au pays natal*. L'Harmattan, 2012.

Cibalabala, Mutshipayi K., editor. *Le drame d'un intellectuel tiraillé entre discours occidental et discours africain: Mélanges offerts au Professeur Georges Ngal à l'occasion de son quatre-vingtième anniversaire*. L'Harmattan, 2014.

Conrad, Joseph. *Heart of Darkness*. Norton Critical Edition, W. W. Norton, 2016.

Dehont, Clarisse. *Des surhommes et des hommes: Regards croisés des stéréotypes à propos de l'Afrique et de l'Africain, de la littérature belge à la littérature congolaise*. 2012. U Laval, Quebec, PhD dissertation.

Derrida, Jacques. *L'écriture et la différence*. Points, 2014.

Diderot, Denis. *Jacques le fatalist et son maître*. Le Livre de Poche, 2019.

Kane, Cheikh Hamidou. *L'aventure ambiguë*. Julliard, 1962.

Kourouma, Ahmadou. *Les soleils des indépendances*. Éditions du Seuil, 1970.

Ladipo, Duro. *Oba Waja (The King Is Dead)*. Translated by Ulli Beier. Soyinka, pp. 74–89.

Le Lay, Maëline. "Entre revolution et utopie: La littérature gestuelle de *Giambatista Viko; ou Le viol du discours africaine*: Une littérature populaire." *Aura d'une écriture: Hommage à Georges Ngal*, edited by Maurice Mpala-Lutebele Amuri, L'Harmattan, 2011, pp. 85–101.

Lodge, David. *Changing Places: A Tale of Two Campuses*. Penguin Books, 1979.

———. *Small World*. Penguin Books, 1995.

Michel, Jean-Claude. *The Black Surrealists*. Peter Lang, 2000.

Miller, Christopher L. *Impostors: Literary Hoaxes and Cultural Authenticity*. U of Chicago P, 2018.

Mirandola, Giovanni Pico della. *De hominis dignitate*. S. Berlusconi, 1994.

———. *Oration on the Dignity of Man*. Translated and edited by Francesco Borghese, Michael Papio, and Massimo Riva, Cambridge UP, 2016.

Mudimbe, Valentin-Yves. "L'affaire *Giambatista Viko*: La mise au point de Mudimbe." Cibalabala, p. 261.

———. "L'affaire *Giambatista Viko*: La mise au point de Mudimbe." *Zaïre-Hebdomadaire*, no. 376, 1975, p. 52.

———. *Entre les eaux: Un prêtre, la revolution*. Présence africaine, 1973.

Ngal, Georges (*see also* Ngal, Mbwil a Mpang). *Aimé Césaire, un homme à la recherche d'une patrie*. 1975. Rev. 2nd ed., Présence Africaine, 1994.

———. *Giambatista Viko; ou, Le viol du discours africain*. Modern Language Association of America, 2021.

———. *Œuvre critique: Articles, communications, interviews, préfaces et études sur Commandes des organisms internationaux 1970–2009*. L'Harmattan, 2009. 2 vols.

Ngal, Mbwil a Mpang (*see also* Ngal, Georges). *L'errance*. 1979. Présence Africaine, 1999.

———. *Giambatista Viko; ou, Le viol du discours africain*. Alpha-Omega, 1975.

———. "Literary Creation in Oral Civilizations." Translated by Richard M. Berrong. *New Literary History*, vol. 8, no. 3, 1977, pp. 335–44.

Ouologuem, Yambo. *Le devoir de la violence*. Éditions du Seuil, 1968.

———. *Lettre à la France nègre*. Serpente à Plumes, 2003.

———. *Les mille et une bibles du sexe*. Vents d'Ailleurs, 2015.

Revel, Jean-François. *Ni Marx ni Jésus: La nouvelle revolution mondiale est commencée aux États-Unis*. 1970. Rev. ed., J'ai Lu, 1973.

Sembène, Ousmane. *Xala*. Présence Africaine, 1976.

Semujanca, Josias. "La mémoire transculturelle comme fondement du sujet africain chez Mudimbe et Ngal." *Tangence*, no. 75, 2004, pp. 15–39.

Soyinka, Wole. *Death and the King's Horseman*. *Death and the King's Horseman*, edited by Simon Gikandi, Norton Critical Edition, W. W. Norton, 1994, pp. 1–64.

Stanley, Henry Morton. *The Congo and the Founding of Its Free State: A Story of Work and Exploration*. Harper and Brothers, 1885.

———. *In Darkest Africa*. 1890. Charles Scribner's Sons, 1913.

———. *Through the Dark Continent*. 1878. Dover, 2011. 2 vols.

Tansi, Sony Labou. *La vie et demie*. Points, 1998.

Ungureanu, Delia. *From Paris to Tlön: Surrealism as World Literature*. Bloomsbury Academic, 2018.

Vico, Giambattista. *New Science*. Translated by David Marsh, Penguin Books, 1999.

———. *La scienza nuova*. *Biblioteca della letterature Italiana*, Pianetascuola / Einaudi, www.letteraturaitaliana.net/pdf/Volume_7/t204.pdf.

Wilde, Oscar. *The Artist as Critic: Critical Writings of Oscar Wilde*. Edited by Richard Ellmann, Random House, 1969.

Note on the Text

Giambatista Viko was originally published in 1975 under the author's then-current name, Mbwil a Mpang Ngal, by Éditions Alpha-Omega in Lubumbashi, Republic of Zaire. In 1984, the novel was republished in Paris by Hatier, in a series entitled Monde Noir Poche that was directed by Jacques Chevrier, a specialist in francophone literature at the Sorbonne. The present edition uses the text of the 1984 edition. Since 2003, the novel has been published by the Paris-based publisher L'Harmattan in a series entitled Encres Noires, using the plates from the Hatier edition but with the author's given name restored to Georges.

GEORGES NGAL

Giambatista Viko; ou, Le viol du discours africain

Première Partie

I

...Pourquoi ce cercle infernal dans lequel on nous enferme ? En sortir ? Par quel sortilège ? Si impossible n'est pas français,[1] possible n'est pas plus français que nègre ! Diable ! Quel saint invoquer ?

— L'avion vient de se poser. Il faut que tu sois la première à l'aérogare. Chaque minute vaut de l'or, il ne faut pas la perdre. Une amitié, lorsqu'elle vient d'un Européen, est d'un prix inestimable. Je tiens à ce que nous soyons les premiers à lui serrer la main.

Elle fonce vite vers l'aérogare. Brûlant le règlement qui interdit aux non-officiels d'entrer dans le salon d'honneur, elle arrive la première. Le ciel est radieux. Sirbu esquisse un large sourire et, d'un geste de la main, salue la cohue venue l'accueillir. Mme Giambatista lui serre longuement la main et lui transmet les salutations de son mari empêché par des obligations professionnelles. Elle a soin de décliner son identité :

1. A favorite saying of Napoleon Bonaparte's to encourage his troops in the face of heavy odds.

— Madame Giambatista !

— Ce n'est que partie remise, chère Madame ; je savoure déjà les heureux moments de collaboration que je passerai avec votre distingué mari. Soleil noir que l'Afrique a l'honneur de compter aujourd'hui parmi les étoiles les plus brillantes que l'humanité ait jamais connues !

...Pourquoi ce cercle infernal dans lequel nous, écrivains nègres, sommes emmurés ? La phrase de Revel me revient, obsédante. Le roman commencé il y a deux ans n'avance pas ; les idées s'enlisent. « Ils n'ont pas de public. Leurs masses sont analphabètes. S'ils écrivent, c'est pour faire revivre un passé révolu, auréolé du titre pompeux d'âge d'or. »[2] Rousseauisme anachronique. Affirmation d'une identité toujours méconnue. Ceux qui tentent d'en sortir, étendent des platitudes destinées en pâture aux pontes parisiens attardés. Plus je rumine ces idées, acceptées sans discussion, plus je me paralyse.

Moi qui ai juré d'être le Chateaubriand de l'Afrique,[3] je vois l'horizon se boucher. Pourtant la plume m'attire

---

2. A quotation from the French journalist and philosopher Jean-François Revel.

3. In *La Génie du christianisme* (1802), the Romantic writer François-René de Chateaubriand included two novellas about noble savages in North America, inspired by his travels there.

irrésistiblement. Des journées entières, je n'arrive pas à écrire une seule ligne. Cependant je me console à la pensée de savoir que Flaubert avait mis cinq ans pour écrire *Madame Bovary*. Pourquoi n'y parviendrais-je pas, moi ? Même s'il me fallait mettre dix, quinze ? Mais le nombre d'années de travail ne fait pas un écrivain. On naît écrivain, comme on dit, *nascuntur poetae, fiunt oratores* !

Je parais exclu du royaume des lettres. La pensée d'un constat d'échec par la critique ajoute à mon angoisse une indéfinissable sensation de dépit et d'impuissance.

J'ai toujours cru que l'écriture apportait une singulière réponse à l'existence. Toujours vu un instrument de libération, la solution à mes drames. La porte de ce royaume qui libère, délivre, me semble définitivement fermée. Maudit soit ce cercle infernal paralysant. Mais si l'idée du cercle était un guet-apens ? Cette forme toujours « originale », « spécifique » de juger les Africains ? Renoncer à la plume, n'est-ce pas tomber dans ce piège tendu perpétuellement par les Occidentaux ? Cette nouvelle manière d'envisager l'écho des paroles de Revel me remonte le moral. L'écriture m'apparaît de nouveau comme ce délicieux havre de jouissances. Lieu où se résolvent les conflits. Miroir de la réconciliation avec nous-mêmes et avec les autres. Sortie de nous-mêmes vers les autres. Prise sur l'altérité. Lieu insondable où l'on se perd, tel le poète maudit,[4] pour se retrouver. Quel écrivain n'a pas cherché cette négativité ! Rimbaud, victime offerte à tous les alcools de la vie ; Baudelaire, une loque humaine ; Nerval, porte béante où tous les rêves affluent. L'écrivain africain!...

— Giambatista, que fais-tu ? Tu m'as l'air complètement égaré ? A quoi rêves-tu ? s'écrie ma femme, en me secouant les bras.

— Oh ! Oui... Je pensais!...

— Sirbu est arrivé, rayonnant. Il te connaît de réputation et a prononcé à ton endroit des paroles exquises qui m'ont remué le cœur. Il faut mettre à profit ce premier contact pour l'avoir avec nous.

— C'est à nous de le baptiser. Tu sais ce qu'il faut faire. Pas une minute à perdre. Demain il sera des nôtres au dîner.

Tu veilleras à mettre en évidence mes deux essais sur l'art d'écrire. De la poudre aux yeux ! Rien de tel que les premières impressions. Je m'arrangerai pour que ce repas qui sera un régal des sens soit aussi celui de l'esprit. Dans notre corps professoral, ils ont tellement peu d'imagination que c'est un véritable plaisir pour moi de mener la

---

4. A dissolute, antisocial writer, such as the poets Arthur Rimbaud (1854–91) and Charles Baudelaire (1821–67) and the visionary novelist Gérard de Nerval (1808–55).

conversation. L'essentiel est de passer pour un brillant causeur. Bien peser les mots. Quelques traits d'esprit placés au bon endroit... Sirbu est à nous.

— As-tu songé, chéri, que demain c'est aussi l'anniversaire du jour de ton doctorat ? On pourrait inviter également, pour cette première rencontre avec Sirbu, le cher Niaiseux. Cela contribuerait à le sortir de sa solitude.

— Excellente idée ! Mais je vois plus loin. C'est le meilleur parrain que nous puissions imaginer pour Sirbu. Niaiseux qui m'appelle respectueusement Maître est le gars qui me comprend à demi-mot. Avec lui la conversation est un pique-nique. Parfait. Pense de quelle adoration le Maître jouit auprès de lui.

Je le tiens en estime. C'est un peu mon parfait reflet. D'habitude, j'ai un mépris du Nègre. Mais lui, il a un quart de sang étranger. Un métis comme il y en a tant. Mais ce que j'aime chez lui, c'est cette intuition presque féminine des problèmes ; cet instinct dont parle Bergson qui sait épouser les points de vue ; en somme mon être. Ce plateau qu'il m'avait offert il y a deux ans à l'occasion de mon anniversaire, sur lequel était gravé un beau soleil, c'est symbolique ! Un soleil brillant dans les ténèbres qui couvrent cet Institut. Niaiseux, malgré ce nom ridicule, par son amitié pour moi — oh, je ne crois pas beaucoup à l'amitié — par son identification à mon système, est un de ces hommes qui ne peuvent vivre sans l'image d'un autre auquel ils s'identifient. Si nous avons tant de succès auprès de quelques étrangers qui sont avec nous, c'est parce qu'ils se retrouvent en nous. L'Europe, la vieille Europe ! Elle s'est retirée de chez nous prématurément. Mais elle n'est pas morte. Qui dans l'Institut parmi les Nègres qui parlent africanisation peut atteindre la cheville de Niaiseux ?

— Allô, Niaiseux ! C'est le Maître à l'appareil ! Pourrais-tu être des nôtres demain au dîner important que nous offrons au nouveau venu, M. Sirbu ?

— Bien sûr, Maître ! Juste deux secondes avant que tu me donnes le coup de fil, j'avançais vers l'appareil…

— Ah ! Simple phénomène de télépathie ! Moi, j'y crois mordicus. Bien des phénomènes s'expliquent par elle. L'amour, l'amitié, les centres d'intérêt communs sont des états télépathiques. Je crois que la Science parviendra dans un avenir pas trop lointain à les formuler mathématiquement.

— Maître, vous avez le don du mot juste.[5] Je suis convaincu que bien des problèmes se résoudront par la télépathologie, la parapsychologie et même par la magie.

---

5. Finding the perfect word or phrase was Gustave Flaubert's goal in writing *Madame Bovary* (1856).

— Tu es, Niaiseux, extraordinaire ! Tu as prononcé le mot qui me brûle les lèvres depuis deux ans. Je crois que c'est une expérience qui mettra une trêve au cauchemar que je vis, au souvenir d'une lecture faite il y a deux ans, peu avant la mise en chantier de mon roman. Un homme ne peut vivre éternellement de souvenirs, il lui faut à un certain moment regarder tout autour de lui ce qui se passe. Et comme par enchantement, tu me mets sur la piste. La magie, fille de la sorcellerie ! Cette manière de dire comme le rappelle R. Firth,[6] qui est le discours propre aux sociétés primitives. Instance où se manifeste le refoulé social. Discours idéologique, la sorcellerie ! Lieu où des oppositions cachées, des contradictions latentes sont restituées. Ce discours, il me faut l'apprivoiser. Quel qu'en soit le prix ! L'écho des paroles de Revel ont fait de moi une sorte de refoulé. Toute parturition littéraire m'est devenue douloureuse. Ma réputation de soleil noir vogue à travers la planète, mais celle de l'écrivain tarde à prendre des assises. Seul le discours intérieur à l'Afrique pourra libérer le mien, enchaîné par un de ces sophismes dont seuls les Occidentaux ont l'art. Il existe une vie souterraine en nous. Le freudisme l'a apprise aux Occidentaux ; les primitifs, eux, ne l'ont jamais ignorée.

---

6. In *The Tongues of Men* (1937), the British linguist J. R. Firth explored the social roots of language in early societies.

Depuis des temps immémoriaux la vie intérieure des individus comme celle des sociétés est réglée par cette instance inférieure que l'Europe commence à peine à redécouvrir.

— Maître, j'ai toujours dit, que vous étiez né trop tôt, avec un siècle d'avance sur notre temps. Apprivoiser le discours africain pour libérer le discours occidental paralysé, refoulé, me paraît vraiment génial !

— Mais attention ! Pas d'ambiguïté ! Je suis de la race qu'on ne peut assimiler aux écrivains africains ordinaires. Nous n'avons de commun que le biologique. Ma place se trouverait à Paris, à Genève. C'est un accident de l'histoire qui m'a fait naître en Afrique. Recours n'est pas assimilation. Picasso, Juan Gris, Liptchiz se sont entourés de masques nègres uniquement dans le but de définir leurs intentions esthétiques ; un Apollinaire proclame sa volonté d'aller vers les fétiches de Guinée et d'Afrique.[7] S'y méprendra qui voudra. Un moyen est un moyen. Ne pas perdre cela de vue.

Accoucher d'un roman ! C'est en effet tenir un discours occidental. C'est évoluer dans l'espace visuel. Faire évoluer un récit dans la dimension spatio-temporelle.

---

7. In Paris in the early 1900s, the Cubist artists Pablo Picasso, Juan Gris, and Jacques Lipchitz drew inspiration from African sculpture, as did the poet and art critic Guillaume Apollinaire, who coined the term *cubism*.

Carcan qui limite étrangement la liberté de l'écrivain ; les possibilités du discours. Le pouvoir du mot très amoindri perd de cette efficacité que lui connaît l'univers magique de l'oralité.

Le mot prononcé « donne le pouvoir sur la chose nommée ; l'image d'argile représente l'ennemi que l'on tue en le transperçant d'une aiguille ». Il faudrait une *Scienza nuova* pour redécouvrir ces puissances spirituelles que l'univers technologique a perdues et que les sociétés orales désinvoltement appelées primitives, ont conservées.[8] Puissance et faculté de déchiffrer le langage enfoui dans les profondeurs du symbolisme ; de décrypter les intentions malveillantes de l'ennemi. Les secrets découverts constituaient des grandes épiphanies du divin sous le voile des environnements : domaine essentiellement du voyant.

— Votre enfance a baigné dans cet univers !

— Mais nous avons été très tôt arrachés et plongés dans celui de l'écrit. Nous avons besoin de le redécouvrir. L'espace acoustique ou plus exactement audio-visuel. Celui du conteur ! Quelle richesse indéfinie ! Quelle liberté dans l'évolution du récit ! Aucune rigidité pareille à celle du roman ! Véritable cercle infernal, l'espace romanesque ! Je rêve d'un roman sur le modèle du conte. D'un

---

8. Viko is here recalling the *Scienza nuova* (*New Science*) of the original Giambattista Vico.

roman où l'opposition entre diachronie et synchronie s'estompe : où coexistent des éléments d'âges différents. D'un univers cinétique : qui engendre un ordre et s'engendre de lui. Cette fécondation du roman par l'oralité que depuis deux ans je m'efforce de réaliser.

Notre enfance tuée, l'écriture pourrait-elle la récupérer ? Hypothèse réalisable ! L'être a besoin de jouer son existence pour survivre. Mais cela suppose de mimer ces récits, ces fictions, ces tours joués par la gazelle au léopard, qui avaient tissé les fibres de notre prime enfance ; de savoir jusqu'où le discours peut faire retour en arrière pour rejoindre ce que, par une éducation précocement bénédictine,[9] nous avons irrémédiablement perdu ; de s'identifier simultanément aux discours de la tortue, du lièvre, de la jeune fille poursuivie par l'ogresse ; insidieusement à celui du lion, de la vieille femme aux neuf ventres ; à celui du public de clair de lune, maître du rejet, de l'exclusion, de la réprobation et de l'approbation ; d'intégrer les multiples lignes de force d'ordonnancement et d'éructation des enveloppes, des procédures de contrôles du discours du conteur ; d'imprimer au récit le rythme par une gibecière magique. Veux-tu comprendre l'écriture rêvée ? Il en va d'elle comme de la jeune fille Nsole, paralytique de nais-

---

9. The Benedictine monastic order had sent many missionaries to the Belgian Congo, and the order's schools retained a considerable role after independence.

sance, choyée par son père à tel point que celui-ci n'aimerait avoir que des filles. Un jour, alors que sa mère était sur le point d'accoucher, son père décide de partir pour un village lointain, appelé par une palabre. Avant le départ il intime l'ordre à sa femme de conserver l'enfant à la naissance si c'est une fille ; de le tuer dans le cas contraire. Le jour venu, la femme met au monde des jumeaux. Elles les cache soigneusement. Au retour de son mari, elle les présente comme des garçons de service. Mais un jour, absents du toit paternel, ils sont trahis par Nsole. Furieux d'avoir été trompé, le père décide de les tuer. Ils sont informés mystérieusement alors qu'ils sont encore loin du village de tout ce qui se tramait contre eux. Aussi se rendent-ils chez la femme du chef du village qui leur donne deux bouteilles à placer dans un coin du toit de la maison. Elles deviendront des livres de prière qu'ils emporteront partout avec eux.

Cependant un jour, le père se saisit du cadet des jumeaux et le livre à ses frères comme du gibier. Plongé dans un fût d'huile bouillante, l'aîné le sauve. Au même instant, leur sœur tuée par leur mère pour trahison, est réveillée au cimetière. Le père à son tour prend la place dans la casserole.

Magie. Tauromachie. Cannibalisme. Merveilleux. Surprise. Traîtrise. Code de l'art africain !

— Mais le roman contemporain semble avoir redécouvert cette liberté que vous recherchez !

— Illusion ! La vie est faite d'illusions. Détruire l'espace balzacien n'est pas tout.[10] L'écrivain contemporain n'est pas allé jusqu'au bout de son entreprise. Il n'est pas parvenu à se débarrasser entièrement du carcan-personnage et du carcan-espace-temps.

— En somme une liberté absolue que vous revendiquez ?

— Pas nécessairement. Personne ne peut échapper au carcan-espace-temps. Mais le maîtriser ! Voilà le vrai problème.

— Vous estimez qu'ils ont mené leur tentative à mi-chemin.

— Oui ! L'avenir du roman est dans la maîtrise de cette donnée. J'y travaille. Arriver à l'abolir ou plus exactement à créer l'illusion de l'abolition, tel est le point de concentration de tous mes efforts. Je suis sur le point d'y parvenir. Le poète Aimé Césaire, jouant au mage africain, suggère timidement cette illusion.

> « Je me souviens de la fameuse peste qui aura lieu
> en l'an 3000 il n'y avait pas eu d'étoile
> annoncière mais seulement la terre en un
> flot sans galettes pétrissantes d'espace

---

10. Referring to the realistic portrayal of ordered social life typified by Honoré de Balzac's panoramic series of novels, *La comédie humaine* (1830–48).

un pain d'herbe et de réclusion
frappe paysan frappe
le premier jour les oiseaux mourront
le second jour les poissons échoueront
le troisième jour les animaux sortiront des bois »[11]

Simple exercice grammatical, peut-être ! Jeu d'esprit ? Mais l'illusion créée par la magie est réussie. Le poète abolit la distinction classique entre le passé, le présent et le futur et s'installe dans une sorte d'éternité. André Breton cherchait ce « point de l'esprit d'où la vie et la mort, le réel et l'imaginaire, le passé et le futur, le communicable et l'incommunicable, le haut et le bas, cessent d'être perçus contradictoirement ».[12] Le surréaliste français a formulé la théorie, à nous de l'illustrer. Les poètes sont en quelque sorte en avance sur nous.

Cercle infernal. Espace-temps ! Le vrai problème réside dans son contrôle et sa maîtrise. Ce n'est pas par le rationalisme rationnel que nous le maîtriserons.

Un conte ce n'est pas ce que tu crois. Il n'est pas en dehors du conteur. Celui-ci est à la fois l'espace scénique ; l'acteur ; le public ; le récit. Un romancier qui réaliserait tous ces éléments ! Quelle performance.

---

11. From Aimé Césaire's surrealistic 1961 poem "À l'Afrique" (*Complete Poetry* 408).

12. Breton, *Second manifeste* 154.

— Une telle littérature est-elle possible ? Si elle l'était, je l'appellerais « littérature gestuelle » comme l'on parle de « l'art gestuel », « de la peinture gestuelle ».

— Vous avez toujours voulu vous engager dans des voies informelles. Cette fois, il me semble que vos recherches vont droit vers l'échec, car une littérature gestuelle ne peut déboucher que sur l'annihilation de la notion même de littérature. Si la peinture gestuelle — « art libéré de contraintes techniques, d'images prédéterminées et de considérations esthétiques » —, a été possible, une littérature gestuelle est irréalisable. Je me rappelle ce qu'écrit Margit Rowell : « Le langage pictural de l'Occident était élaboré selon les nécessités de la représentation de l'objet. Abolir l'objet d'une manière aussi radicale, c'est abolir certaines conventions de dessin, couleur, composition, inventées en fonction des rapports traditionnels entre l'artiste et son objet... Abolir l'objet, c'est encore abolir l'espace de l'objet et l'espace est un élément déterminant de la peinture. C'est abolir les composantes de la vision spatiale traditionnelle tels que la perspective, les plans, la profondeur, les proportions, l'étendue, la composition, l'organisation, l'articulation, les rapports des formes avec un fond ou avec d'autres formes. »[13] On

---

13. From *La peinture, le geste, l'action: L'existentialisme en peinture* (10). In it, Rowell championed "la peinture gestuelle," which is concerned more with the act of painting than with the result.

sait que les tenants de cette nouvelle forme de peinture étaient obsédés par une quête d'authenticité. Mais je crois que l'esthétique fut sacrifiée.

— Qu'est-ce que l'esthétique ? A une époque où la laideur aussi a ses beautés ? Ne sais-tu pas que ce qu'on appelle le beau sexe a des leçons utiles à nous donner. Toute femme au monde, la « laide » comme la « moins laide » a un admirateur. L'esthétique est fille de l'éducation et de la culture...

Ma femme intervient. Je raccroche. Au dehors le soleil s'est donné rendez-vous avec la nature. Éclat. Dorure. Beauté. Symphonie des couleurs. Les oiseaux sentent comme par instinct la disparition prochaine de l'astre radieux. Les gris-gris poussent des crissements repris en chœur par les croassements des poules et les roucoulements des pigeons.[14] La nature entière me paraît complice par son silence contre moi, contre mes recherches. L'optimisme retrouvé ne me donne pas la maîtrise de l'écriture. De l'espace-temps. Tout semble m'avoir fui. Les énergies latentès s'obstinent à ne pas se réveiller.

— La dernière et la bonne ? Veux-tu l'apprendre ?

— Oui ! De quoi s'agit-il ?

---

14. Gris-gris are protective amulets that clatter together when worn around the waist.

— Une publication de X dans la *Revue des Sciences de l'homme* ![15]

— Cela allonge donc sa liste ! Je dois la lire. Éviter surtout d'en parler aux membres de l'Institut. Il ne faut surtout pas que les illusions dont se nourrit cet énergumène prennent de jour en jour en lui des racines profondes. Mon indignation est viscérale. Une seule personne dont on doit parler ! Niaiseux comprend. A l'instant où je te parle, il me sent par télépathie. Je ne veux pas agir directement. Soyons fins. Je joue à l'opération séduction. Niaiseux et tous mes adulateurs coiffés du titre pompeux de Coopérants se chargent du reste… Je suis seulement le souffleur. Comme dans une pièce de théâtre. La face est sauvée. Cela lui coûtera cher de prétendre se mesurer au Maître. Il ne faut pas beaucoup d'astuces. Un sourire narquois des Coopérants à son passage. Répété plusieurs fois. Un isolement progressif. Le cancer des solitudes fera le reste.

— Allô, Giambatista ! Olibrinus au bout du fil ![16]

— Oui, je reconnais cette voix timbrée et sonore.

---

15. A reference to the *Revue des sciences humaines*, a leading French social science journal, in which Ngal himself had recently published an article, "Le théâtre d'Aimé Césaire: Une dramaturgie de la décolonisation."

16. The name Olobrinus likely evokes Olibrius, who was briefly installed as a puppet Roman emperor in 472 CE; in French tradition his name came to signify an empty-headed braggart.

— On m'annonce la dernière publication de X. Infecte. Comment cette revue dont la renommée scientifique est internationale a-t-elle eu la faiblesse de publier un tel navet. La langue à peine maîtrisée. Tu devrais donner dans le numéro 10 la réplique pour relever le défi et faire taire définitivement cet élément!...

— Je le vois avec d'autres yeux. Le seul étranger qui est avec lui jubile à l'instant. Tous deux se disent satisfaits de l'allure que prend sa renommée, plutôt sa réputation « scientifique », entre guillemets. Tu sais ce qu'il faut faire. La conspiration du silence. Tous les copains comprennent le jeu. A toi de jouer.

« Pourquoi aujourd'hui, tous ces visages, d'habitude détendus, me boudent-ils ? Même Olibrinus, c'est à peine s'il ose me jeter un regard ! Des petits groupes se forment. Quand je passe, silence soudain. Des lèvres s'étirent. J'entends des soupirs... Tout semble conspirer. »

— C'est parfait. Pas meilleure leçon que celle-là. Tu as le don, non seulement de voir la réalité avec d'autres yeux mais aussi de te dédoubler. Un parfait orchestrateur. Inspirateur-Souffleur. Acteur. Spectateur. En somme l'illustration de tes recherches. Un génie tel que toi devrait faire partie du Club de Rome.

— C'est exact. Tu as toujours le mot juste. J'y pense sérieusement. La demande est rédigée. Comme mes recherches s'inscrivent dans le prolongement de son rapport, il n'y a aucune difficulté à y entrer par la grande porte.

Aurelio Peccei ; Alexander King ; Hugo Thiemann ; Eduard Pestel ; Saburō Ōkita ; Adeoye Lombo ; Adam Schaff ; quel aréopage ![17]

« Monsieur GIAMBATISTA, des génies de votre classe, ont leur place indiquée dans notre club. Nous sommes au courant de vos recherches. Un soleil qui recule tous les jours les limites de l'obscurité épaisse qui couvre le continent noir, brille parmi nous et éclaire chacun des membres d'un éclat presque aveuglant. Des hommes de votre taille on en compte un par siècle. Votre contribution fera avancer nos études d'un pas de géant. Une de nos conclusions étant : "Nous déclarons enfin que toute tentative délibérée pour parvenir à un équilibre rationnel et stable grâce à des programmes concertés — plutôt que de laisser au hasard ou aux catastrophes le soin de rétablir un équilibre compromis — dépendra en dernier ressort d'une révision profonde des valeurs et des objectifs propres aux individus, aux nations et à l'ensemble du

17. The Italian industrialist Aurelio Peccei and the Scottish scientist Alexander King founded the Club of Rome in 1968, bringing together politicians, economists, scientists, and business leaders from around the world to study global problems. Viko now imagines being inducted into the club and rehearses his acceptance speech.

monde",[18] il vous appartient, distingué Collègue, d'opérer cette révision des valeurs. »

— Merci, Monsieur le Président et chers Collègues. Les paroles de l'éminent et distingué savant, M. Aurélio Peccei, me rendent un peu confus. L'honneur qui m'échoit aujourd'hui, rejaillit en fait sur tous les membres du club. Le soleil ne luit pas pour lui-même. Il réchauffe. Il brûle. Il consume tout ce qui l'entoure. Ce langage imagé vous donne une faible idée de ce qu'est mon rôle parmi vous. Le rapport du Comité exécutif se termine par ces mots : « Nous voudrions enfin, et c'est notre dernier souhait, inviter chaque homme à rentrer en luimême : il lui faut sonder ses valeurs et ses fins tout autant que ce monde qu'il aspire changer. A l'une et l'autre tâche, il faut se consacrer entièrement. Mais en fin de compte, l'important n'est pas tant de savoir si la vie vaut la peine d'être vécue. »[19] C'est tout un programme. Aux âmes bien nées, aux étoiles dont la lumière brille d'un éclat pur, tels que nous, appartient de changer l'homme. Nous sommes à un tournant où le seul langage des statistiques, la seule poésie des chiffres ne suffisent à sauver l'humanité. Les prophéties sur les limites de la

---

18. From the Club of Rome's bestselling study *The Limits to Growth* (Meadows et al. 195).

19. Meadows et al. 197.

croissance, sur la terre cultivable, l'atmosphère, les ressources naturelles jettent l'alarme. Leur écho rappelle étrangement les cris de Malthus.[20] Et pourtant la terre continue de tourner. Va-t-elle vers son suicide ? A chaque étape les hommes s'adaptent à la situation. Le drame de l'humanité réside, bien sûr, dans les limites et les possibilités de la croissance continue. En dernier ressort, c'est un problème d'espace. Nous nous inquiétons de celui de demain. L'inquiétude tue. La prescience étouffe. La révision des valeurs que nous rêvons est plus qu'un problème de réaménagement de l'espace. Éminents Collègues, vous me permettrez de prendre d'abord quelques précautions oratoires. L'espace est tellement pollué que les mots ont perdu leur véritable sens.

Entre savants nulle équivoque. Quelques têtes bien-pensantes de la planète donnent à ce mot un sens qui nous oriente dangereusement. Je pense à *l'Homme unidimensionnel* de H. Marcuse.[21] Aucun savant n'accepte aujourd'hui ce sophisme scientiste qui nous enferme dans le circuit fermé production-consommation, base de notre aliénation. C'est là voir les choses avec des œillères. Re-

---

20. The English economist Thomas Malthus (1766–1834) calculated that population growth would inevitably outstrip available resources.

21. The German American philosopher Herbert Marcuse's influential 1964 book criticizes both capitalism and communism for repressing individuality in favor of a totalizing ideology.

tomber finalement dans les insuffisances que notre club a pour mission de dépasser. A l'espace unidimensionnel, je vous suggère de substituer l'espace pluridimensionnel, composé de plusieurs couches superposées. Au circuit production-consommation s'est superposé le circuit Sexe-consommation qui appartient à une autre hiérarchie des valeurs. Ce deuxième circuit hante tellement notre espace qu'il nous est impossible de percevoir l'échelle réelle des valeurs. Je relève à titre d'exemple, exposé à tout venant sur la devanture d'un kiosque à NEW YORK, MONTRÉAL, etc., les magazines suivants :

CONFIDENCES
DUDE
ALL MAN
SENSUOUS
WILLCAT
FOR MEN ONLY
SIR
MR.
PLAY-BOY
PLAYERS
MADAME
MALADE
SEXTUS
SEXE FOU
SEXPRESS « La putain la plus courue en ville. Un sein »
EXTASE
LESBO

SEXTRA
PARTENAIRES
SEXY
SECRET
ELLE
LUI
POSES D'ART
NYMPHO
MIDNIGHT
MINUIT « Le parapluie érotique »
ENCORE
ALMANACH DU SEXE
PORNO
BISEXUS
CONFIDENCES
INSEIDE NEWS
PLAYGIRLS
ADAM
GIRLS AROUND THE WORLD
MAN TO MAN
OUI

On a tellement tout sexué, y compris la femme, que l'espèce humaine connaît aujourd'hui une troisième dimension sexuelle. L'on parle de « l'homme trisexuel ». Cet être monstrueux qu'aucune loi scientifique ne prévoit semble défier la Science ! Ce nouveau « paramètre » de l'espace nous place devant nos responsabilités d'hommes de science. Il s'empare de la télévision, du cinéma, de la radio, de tous les mass media. Il est omniprésent. Son absence est encore une présence. Le nombre d'accidents mortels (le sexe et le cœur) est inouï. Les statistiques indiquent que le nombre de cardiaques a quintuplé en deux ans. Phénomène inquiétant.

Cependant devant l'apparition soudaine de ce troisième homme, la science ne devrait pas être désemparée. Elle se doit de relever le défi. Selon mes premières intuitions — les vérités les plus sublimes sont nées de l'intuition — ce troisième homme nous révélerait une tendance fondamentale de notre être. L'homme, en désirant la femme, exprimerait le désir (refoulé) de rejoindre le sein maternel, espace premier, primordial. L'explosion du sexe est donc un dynamisme normal. Notre époque a donc mieux compris cet attrait nostalgique que les périodes antérieures. Certains pourraient croire qu'il s'agirait alors de laisser l'érotisme se débrider pour rejoindre un nirvana indifférencié, espace sans profondeur, ni épaisseur. Rien de tout cela ! Ni Nirvana dissolvant les essences, ni indifférenciation primordiale, ni un Impersonnel, ou un Universel qui aurait pour attributs le non-être, le vide absolu. Il y a ici plénitude ; au contraire : plénitude en un point primordial. Imaginez cent mille coups de téléphone reçus au même moment par un seul appareil ; par un seul individu ! On serait alors en présence d'une totalité dans la multiplicité. Multiplicité maîtrisée par l'unité. Chacun des coups de téléphone y gardant son individualité, on comprend pourquoi l'écriture, la littérature gestuelle qui a pour mission de rendre le mouvement de l'unité primordiale, est l'expression la plus haute et la plus sublime de notre rapport à cet espace individualisé par l'écrivain. Le geste incarne une plénitude, la rend visible, la rend sensible dans un mouvement unique.

Espace primordial. Temps primordial. Rythme pur. Dynamisme. Flux et reflux vibratoires. Nos concepts gauchissent la réalité quand nous y appliquons les catégories aristotéliciennes d'avant et d'après. Antérieur à son extériorisation, il est parole repliée sur elle-même ; modulation avant de s'extérioriser en discours. Il est vain de vouloir lui coller un présent et lui chercher un passé. Mon éminent collègue, Merleau-Ponty, a raison, quand il parle du temps comme pur rapport avec les choses, ayant ses racines dans le présent.[22]

— Mais Giambatista, ce temps n'a-t-il pas ses racines dans le passé des parents ?[23]

— J'admets l'hérédité, Olibrinus. Mais l'hérédité n'est pas le temps. C'est le poids d'un autre devenu présent en moi. Il n'est pas succession d'instants. Il reste vrai que les parents sont pure relation. Il faut se défaire des catégories habituelles. Espace et temps ici se confondent. Rythmes

22. The French philosopher Maurice Merleau-Ponty (1908–61) wrote extensively about the historical and embodied quality of experience.

23. Here Viko's friend Olobrinus, still on the telephone, interrupts Viko's imagined acceptance speech in Rome.

et vibrations. Nulle dimension, nulle profondeur. N'y chercher que l'immédiateté. Que la relativité. Durée qui s'engendre elle-même. Il te faut, Olibrinus, t'accommoder de ce vocabulaire, de cette tournure de pensée un peu insolite. Mes collègues du club qui m'écoutent avec l'attention la plus soutenue comprennent sans difficulté. Il est vrai que c'est à des savants que je m'adresse. Tiens. Voilà une expérience de maîtrise du temps tentée par un des mes amis, Bernardo, au sud du pays des Apika.[24] Pendant trois mois, il se débarrasse de sa montre pour ne suivre que le mouvement de l'astre radieux. Au bout de quelque temps, il perd la notion de semaine, de mois, d'année. Seule lui reste celle du jour. Mais qu'est-ce que le jour, Olibrinus, dans ce contexte ? Est-ce l'espace compris entre l'apparition de l'aube et la venue de la nuit ? Ou cet espace additionné à la nuit ? Vingt-quatre heures ou douze heures est un choix. Arbitraire. Les Apika vivent leur temps. Ils le maîtrisent. Pour eux, la journée n'est pas avant la nuit ; ni celle-ci avant la journée. Les Esquimaux vivent six mois sans un avant diurne ni un après nocturne. Je sais que l'idéologie ethnocentriste lève déjà les boucliers. Les philosophes Sartre, Buber, Heidegger, Merleau-Ponty vont en guerre contre cette thèse. Mais les arguments décisifs ! Viennent des systèmes

---

24. A tribe in the Amazon.

philosophiques eux-mêmes. Ils se contredisent les uns les autres. Où est la vérité ? Qu'est-ce que la vérité, crache Pilate à celui qui se dit la Vérité incarnée ![25]

A vrai dire, la vérité n'est-elle pas pure relation avec les choses ? Variant avec l'angle de vision que l'on choisit de considérer les choses ? L'idéologie ethnocentriste a vite convaincu les hommes. « Au monde réel, la pensée primitive ou mythique substitue un monde "d'ailleurs" ; à l'espace réel, un espace "vital" et par cela même "sacré", au temps réel, un temps "primordial". Qui décide que tel espace est réel et tel autre non-réel ? C'est l'homme ! Qui confond les deux ? C'est l'homme ! La vérité, chers Collègues du Club, réside dans le choix relationnel.

Ceux que nous appelons primitifs font la leur pour organiser leur existence de cette manière. Nous les « Civilisés » organisons la nôtre suivant nos critères. Les primitifs ont leurs critères. Nous avons les nôtres. Nous nous comportons souvent comme les Scolastiques qui pourfendent l'hégélianisme, le marxisme, en allant chercher des critères chez Thomas d'Aquin au lieu de réfuter Hegel à partir de lui-même.

Une autre comparaison nous révèle la dimension du sophisme dans lequel nous vivons. L'État enferme cer-

---

25 When Jesus is tried by Pontius Pilate and says that everyone who belongs to the truth hears his voice, Pilate retorts, "What is truth?" and allows him to be crucified (John 18.38).

tains individus dans des maisons appelées "asiles des fous".[26] Qui peut nous dire la ligne de démarcation entre l'état d'aliénation et l'état de non aliénation ? Je parie que la planète entière est un asile de fous. Les moins fous abusent des autres.

Il nous faut, chers Éminents Collègues, cher Olibrinus, réviser nos valeurs, notre échelle de valeurs mais, avant cela, nos concepts. Des concepts sûrs et acceptés par tous, voilà la plate-forme commune qui doit accueillir tout dialogue. »

---

26. Here Viko echoes the critique of psychiatry, and of Western rationality in general, by the philosopher Michel Foucault in works such as *Folie et déraison* (1961).

II

Un litre. Deux litres. Je sens mes membres s'alourdir, mon esprit se délier. Oh ! que vois-je ? Une immense boule avec des tentacules. D'elle s'échappent une fumée et des nuages. Des fourmis accouplées à des éléphants ; la terre féconde les nuages. Le lion fraternise avec le chacal ; l'étoile avec la taupe. Éblouissement furieux de la lumière. Buffle contre l'abeille. Mer contre vagues. Jabs des géants.

— Encore un troisième litre. C'est le baptême de la délivrance des Éléments. Qui veut devenir lui-même doit passer par cette étape.

Nous nous engageons dans un couloir souterrain long d'environ deux cents mètres. Nous arrivons dans une cavité. Qui semble servir de charnière. Les murs de la caverne sont tapissés de peau humaine fraîchement garnis. A chaque mètre, est suspendu un crâne. Des ossements humains et animaux entassés pêle-mêle dans les quatre coins de la caverne. Des crânes taillés et ciselés selon un certain art, servent de récipients pour différentes sortes de boissons. Des sceptres pendant çà et là. Un serpent vivant longe la caverne en faisant le tour à une allure de caméléon. Un silence lugubre règne.

Une main me tend une coupe remplie d'un liquide rouge.

— Prends et bois. Tu es des nôtres.

— Non ! dis-je.

— Prends et bois. Tu es des nôtres. Quand on arrive dans la caverne on en sort ou on n'en sort pas !

Les voix se font menaçantes. Je prends la coupe. Puisqu'elle est tirée il faut la boire.[27] Je la bois. Une odeur nauséabonde se répand dans toute la cavité. Des voix aiguës sifflent, alternant avec d'autres plus graves.

Ceux qui t'arrachent à notre univers
Ceux qui t'introduisent dans l'univers de
Ceux qui chaque jour nous tuent à petit feu
Ceux qui paralysent nos énergies au bénéfice de
    l'étranger meurent à jamais par ce sang
    que tu bois.
Malheur à quiconque ose recourir à nous pour
    servir des intérêts étrangers.
A bon entendeur salut !

Les voix reprennent ce refrain sans interruption. Trois fois. Est-ce un délire ? Une hallucination ? Puis tout d'un coup des lumières aveuglantes rouges ; bleues ; jaunes. Obscurité totale. Un masque rouge fortement éclairé

27. Echoing the proverb "Quand le vin est tiré il faut le prendre."

crache des flammes ; suivi de deux autres, puis de trois. Au bout d'un instant toute la caverne est peuplée entièrement de masques. Commence alors une procession. De la caverne vers la sortie. Deux masques géants, soutenus on ne sait par quelle main invisible, ouvrent la marche. Moi, derrière, encadré par deux de chaque côté. Arrivée près de la sortie, la procession fait demi-tour et revient. Puis un crachement général de flammes qui se font de plus en plus vives. Elles s'éteignent soudainement. Les voix reprennent en chœur.

> Ceux qui t'arrachent à notre univers
> Ceux qui t'introduisent dans l'univers de
> Ceux qui chaque jour nous tuent à petit feu
> Ceux qui paralysent nos énergies au bénéfice de
>   l'étranger meurent à jamais par ce sang
>   que tu bois.
> Malheur à quiconque ose recourir à nous pour
>   servir des intérêts étrangers.
> A bon entendeur salut !

Une main me tend encore une coupe.

— Prends et bois. Tu es des nôtres désormais.

Je la saisis de deux mains et la bois. Et me plonge dans un sommeil profond.

Trêve de paroles.

— Allô, Mme Giambatista !

— Olibrinus !

— Qu'est-ce qui se passe ? Je suis accroché au téléphone et n'entends plus la voix de Giambatista. Il semble avoir raccroché ![28]

— Giambatista s'enferme chaque jour à cinq heures dans son bureau avec un monsieur pour une séance de travail. Interdiction formelle d'ouvrir. Attendez qu'ils aient fini.

Je me sens courbaturé. La tête légère. Les épaules lourdes. J'ouvre la fenêtre. Senteurs d'épices et de fleurs sauvages. Signe d'approche de la nuit africaine. Entêtement du soleil qui se refuse à mourir. Dans la cour les poules, les pigeons courent çà et là. A l'horizon un arcenciel tamise les derniers rayons du soleil. Prisme étoilé. Orgie des couleurs. Je ne me rappelle rien de précis. Mon esprit saute d'une idée à l'autre, tel un singe d'une branche à l'autre. Chaque image me retient longuement, me fascine. Je m'extasie. Les extases se succèdent, entrecoupées par des griffes intermittentes de mon chat. Passant devant le miroir adossé à un mur, mes yeux s'ébrouent. Je ne me reconnais pas. Réalité hallucinante ? J'y crois. L'Africain est un halluciné. Rachid Boudjedra a raison de croire en la vertu de l'hallucination.[29] En la vertu de la folie. Nous sommes, nous Africains, des fous.

---

28. In the original edition, this paragraph appears to be spoken by Viko's wife, but this seems to be a printer's error.

29. Rachid Boudjedra (b. 1941) is an Algerian poet, novelist, and critic.

« Folie arborescente. » « Folie qui hurle. »[30] Tout est folie. Rythmes. Danses. Folie phosphorescente. Poésie africaine. Délire collectif. Torrent de débauche. Amour de la vie. Amour de l'amour. Vie en rut.[31] Perpétuel cauchemar. Terreurs nocturnes. Terreurs diurnes, réalités confondues. Nous sommes la vie. Plénitude. L'idée de néant ![32] Invention et stupidité étrangère. Venin mortel. Paysages lointains ? Royaume de l'ignorance. Nostalgie, notre ennemie. Présence, notre être. La mort, notre détente. Rêve. Ivresse. Extase. Nous haïssons les attentes. Les passages. Les arrivées. Les départs. Les démultiplications. Tout est présence.

— Chéri, Olibrinus au téléphone !

— Ah ! Que veux-tu, ces pauvres gens ont besoin de soutien ! Il est vrai que je me sers d'eux. Mes intérêts à l'Institut se portent merveilleusement bien grâce à eux. Si l'amitié, cette sorte de détente entre les humains existe, je dois la leur rendre. Coopérants ! Malgré mes apaisements, l'inquiétude règne toujours parmi eux.

Ma puissance n'est donc pas encore suffisamment reconnue ! Le malheur, dans ce pays, c'est que la rumeur

---

30. These phrases are taken from the works of the Congolese poet Tchicaya U Tam'si and Césaire, whom Georges Ngal compared in his essay "Introduction à une lecture d'*Epitomé* de Tchicaya U Tam'si."

31. A sarcastic play on the title of the romantic song "La vie en rose."

32. Jean-Paul Sartre emphasized the self's struggle against *le néant* in his existentialist magnum opus, *L'être et le néant* (1943).

a autant de consistance que la vérité. La radio-trottoir a autant d'impact que la radio nationale.

— Olibrinus, cher Olibrinus ! Ce n'est qu'une simple rumeur. La convention signée entre les deux pays reste en vigueur. Tu sais, il y a la politique du corbeau, qui clame rauquement tout haut ses menaces, il y a celle de la taupe. Je préfère celle-ci. Je te donne ma parole. Ma protection te suffit.

— Tu es adorable, Giambatista ! Sans toi aucun Coopérant ne saurait survivre. Une vague d'africanisation balaye actuellement le pays. Nous sommes faibles. Un retour au pays, c'est notre mort. Irreclassables. L'inquiétude nous ronge ; c'est notre pain quotidien. Nos nuits sont blanches. Le sommeil n'est plus pour nous qu'un souvenir. Pourtant nous avons servi ce pays ! Nous aurions droit à un minimum de reconnaissance. Toi, tu es notre espoir. Notre respiration.

Prenons le problème sous un autre angle. Celui de la civilisation. La civilisation avec un grand *C*, basée sur la culture humaniste, se meurt de jour en jour. Nous assistons impuissants. Ce pays compterait-il deux intellectuels de ta trempe, l'Occident jubilerait. Toute la colonie des Coopérants te remercie. Je me fais ici son porte-parole.

— Merci. Mais tranquillise-toi. Si ton inquiétude était fondée, pourquoi ce nouvel arrivé que j'accueille demain ?

— Tu connais bien la logique bantoue.[33] Je m'en méfie.

— Moi aussi, je m'en méfie. Elle est déroutante. Je compatis. J'assiste béat à la décivilisation du continent baptisée de tous les noms. Renaissance africaine, négritude, etc. Il s'agit en réalité d'une africanolâtrîe. C'est bien le mot adéquat. Mais crois-moi, tout n'est pas encore perdu.

Les centres culturels occidentaux — épines dorsales pour les Africanolâtres — font tâche d'huile. Ils contribuent à nous rappeler la présence permanente de la culture. Par ailleurs, il leur faudra des siècles pour arriver à promouvoir leurs langues au niveau de « langues de culture »,[34] je veux dire de langues internationales. Calme-toi. Dis à tous tes collègues que je suis avec eux de cœur et d'esprit. Je suis déjà parvenu à arrêter les trois-quarts de…

Allô ? Tu m'écoutes toujours ?

— Bien sûr ! Tes paroles sont de l'or !

---

33. A nonlinear mode of thought, open to seeming contradictions. During the period of decolonization in the 1950s and 1960s, a number of Central African intellectuals sought alternatives to westernization by exploring the ancestral thought world of the region's Bantu peoples.

34. Referring to "Le français, langue de culture," an essay by Léopold Sédar Senghor that discusses the ongoing value of French for decolonized African writers, as the best language in which to construct "un monde nouveau—celui de l'Homme. Un monde idéal et réel en même temps" (840).

— Les prends-tu vraiment au sérieux ? Aujourd'hui, une réforme. Demain, marche arrière. Contradiction sur contradiction. En somme l'illustration la plus parfaite de la logique bantoue. Là où les choses frisent la folie — c'est bien le cas de le dire — quand ils décrètent l'africanolâtrie, c'est alors qu'ils s'occidentalisent à fond. S'en rendent-ils compte ? Sais-tu qu'ils ont tous des immeubles en Occident ? Leurs enfants fréquentent soit des écoles consulaires soit des écoles françaises, belges, anglaises en Europe ? Insensibilité ? Naïveté ? Absence de logique ? Le peuple en est-il dupe ? Je ne le crois pas. C'est te dire, cher Olibrinus, qu'il faut prendre les choses avec philosophie.

En ce qui me concerne, mon choix est clair. Plus exactement il n'y en a pas. Une culture humaniste — gréco-latine — assaisonnée d'une érudition que tout le monde me reconnaît ! Où veux-tu que je la case ? Je ne crois ni au métissage ni à l'intégration des cultures. La juxtaposition ? Possible ! Qui peut marier la logique cartésienne à la logique bantoue ?

On ne mélange pas la boue à la pureté !

— Certains tiers-mondistes proclament que le capitalisme international informe la « nature profonde » des coupeurs de noix de palme de la forêt équatoriale. Comme le social, le culturel, etc., ne s'introduisent pas après coup ; sont déjà là dans la production, ne crois-tu pas en la mort lente de la culture bantoue chez ces pauvres coupeurs ?

— Dans la logique du marxiste léniniste, oui ! C'est notre credo ; celui de tout homme cultivé. Marx. Lénine. Althusser.[35] Nos maîtres à penser. Cependant la rigidité de ce modèle doit inciter à la prudence. Les hétérogénéités locales ont parfois des soubresauts inattendus. Ce qui me fait croire en la possibilité de la juxtaposition des cultures ; en la « marxisation » même du marxisme aujourd'hui. Les paramètres proposés par Marx ne sont pas aussi figés que ne le laissent penser certains tiers-mondistes pressés. Preuve : les lectures multiples de Marx. Aucun lecteur de l'auteur du *Capital* ne peut prétendre avoir dit le dernier mot.

— On reste médusé par la hâte avec laquelle certains baptisent Marx et Lénine dans le Tiers-Monde. Je parie que ceux-ci se remuent dans leurs tombes. Pense un peu à la vague de « bantouisation » du marxisme que connaît le continent actuellement.

— L'essentiel est de trouver un type de lucidité qui dissimule le refus de discuter des vrais problèmes qui se posent aux peuples. Le marxisme est devenu l'opium

35. Louis Althusser (1918–90) was a leading Marxist philosopher in Paris.

au même titre que le football.[36] La diversion. C'est tout un art !

— Aujourd'hui « développement » signifie diversion. La politique est, elle aussi, devenue l'art de créer la diversion. Quelle est la responsabilité de vous autres, intellectuels, dans cette situation ?

— Nous assistons, ahuris, impuissants et même médusés. Les gris-gris jouissent de plus de crédit que nous les intellectuels. Et puis… il faut posséder pour être considéré. Évidences crevantes. Des bourgeois surgis du néant qui constituent cette périphérie dont parle Samir Amin.[37] Leurs avoirs, des Himalayas élevés en quinze ans. Des philistins. Comment les récupérer ? Renverser les valeurs ? L'échelle des valeurs ? Ils sont maintenant dans le circuit mondial. La machine tourne. Le mécanisme est implacable ; loi de l'accumulation élargie du capital. Création d'une plus-value adéquate. Profit. Nécessité de perpétuer le travail aliéné. L'exploitation. Ces cris sont de Herbert Marcuse. On ne peut sauver la Terre dans le cadre du capitalisme. On ne peut développer le Tiers-Monde selon le modèle du capitalisme. La lutte pour une

---

36. Viko applies to Marxism itself the famous assertion by Karl Marx that religion is the opium of the people (Introduction).

37. Samir Amin (1931–2018) was an Egyptian political scientist who coined the term *Eurocentrism*.

extension du monde de la beauté, de la non-violence, du calme est une lutte politique. L'insistance sur ces valeurs, sur la restauration de la terre comme environnement humain n'est pas seulement une idée romantique, esthétique, poétique qui ne concerne que les privilégiés : c'est aujourd'hui une question de survie. Le but, c'est le bien-être par la conquête d'une vie délivrée de la peur, de l'esclavage du salaire, de la violence, de la puanteur, du bruit infernal du monde industriel capitaliste. Il ne s'agit pas de rendre rebelle l'abomination, de cacher la misère, de désodoriser la puanteur, de fleurir les prisons, les banques, les usines ; il ne s'agit pas de purifier la société existante mais de la remplacer.

— Je ne te vois pas mais j'imagine que c'est Herbert Marcuse qui par ta bouche parle ainsi !

— C'est un des maîtres qui m'ont marqué. Mais il a évolué, vois-tu. De même que le moine bénédictin pense par référence à la Bible, à la parole de son Dieu ; moi aussi j'ai mes dieux. Ils ont noms : Marx, Lénine, Althusser, Sartre, Marcuse. Dans la vie, chacun a son dieu.

— Tes dieux semblent habiter le sanctuaire des livres ?

— Marx, Lénine ne sont pas un univers livresque. Ils sont le moteur de l'histoire. Leur doctrine, je veux dire. La marche de l'histoire n'est plus intelligible sans eux.

Notre discussion se poursuit. A bâtons rompus. Le problème de l'écriture revient. Mon renom. Le génie créateur. La matière. Ses résistances. La forme. Le style. Les rêves. Les fantasmes. L'hallucination. L'art. Le travail créateur. La lutte du génie pour imposer au marbre une forme.

Le stylet de Michel-Ange tirant Moïse du néant. L'artiste est dieu. Il conçoit. Il projette. Il imprime ses fantasmes sur la page blanche. Il les cisèle dans la pierre. Il les transporte dans la musique. Il informe la matière. Un démiurge. Je sens revenir à la surface la passion d'écrire. J'interromps la conversation avec Olibrinus.

Les idées grouillent dans ma tête. Affrontement des fantasmes. Corps à corps. Les images semblent affluer toutes à la fois dans le discours. D'autres résistent et restent au seuil. Ma paralysie semble guérie. Mais pourquoi cette précipitation des images ? Toutes veulent être reçues en un seul jet, sans attendre un ordonnancement ? Pourquoi d'autres résistent-elles ? Je sens en moi comme deux puissances contradictoires. L'une libère les fantasmes, l'autre les retient. La première veut les loger tous dans le flux et reflux des phrases. La deuxième s'y oppose et veux les étaler les uns après les autres. Certains fantasmes sont rythmes et vibrations purs ; je ne parviens pas à les fixer malgré toute ma concentration.

Suis-je éveillé ou en rêve ? Non je suis parfaitement lucide. Arrivé maintenant au terme de mon initiation je devrais être capable de cette « littérature gestuelle » rêvée ! Ai-je enfreint quelque interdit ? Peut-être ! Mais qui me le dira ? Le secret est absolu. L'indiscrétion, fatale. Non, ce n'est qu'une impression.

— Allô, Niaiseux !

— Maître !

— Toujours prompt à reconnaître la voix du Maître ! Comment vont les choses ?

— L'opération silence réussit à merveille. A l'Institut il ne trouve personne à qui parler. Même Malawi avec qui il cause habituellement, semble lui tourner le dos. Tu sais ce petit zèbre de Malawi ne manque pas d'ambition. Il supporte mal le succès scientifique de X comme le vôtre d'ailleurs.

Les Nègres sont tous les mêmes. Ils digèrent mal la réussite du voisin. Ne te rappelles-tu pas les nombreuses imprécations que les femmes dans les villages lancent contre leurs voisines quand les poules de celles-ci viennent caqueter dans leurs parcelles ? On l'a entendu, semble-t-il, chuchoter des propos amers !

— Le problème pour Malawi, c'est le manque d'ouverture au dehors. Il a une spécialité où il n'y a pas un souffle d'air quelconque. Il me fait pitié. N'empêche cependant que nous puissions l'utiliser. Contre un ennemi commun on s'allie toujours. Un dîner à la mwambe et tu l'as avec toi.[38] Le tiers de mon salaire est toujours investi dans les dîners que j'offre. Demain, c'est le tour de Sirbu d'être accueilli. Tu seras des nôtres d'ailleurs.

— Maître, tout cela est parfait. Mais il faut arriver à battre ce zèbre en vous imposant par une série de publications. L'illusion de crédit dont il semble jouir auprès des autorités vient de ce qu'il fait croire qu'il publie beaucoup.

— Illusion qui ne durera plus guère longtemps. Mon étoile ne peut souffrir une quelconque subordination, surtout à un nègre. Le retard dans mes publications n'est que passager. Le « décollage », comme disent les psychanalystes, ne va pas tarder.[39] J'avais longtemps constitué une anthologie de textes sur la création littéraire. Des morceaux de tous les génies que l'humanité ait produits. Je m'en suis imprégné. Le phénomène d'osmose doit jouer. De génie à génie, cela va de soi. Un génie s'identifiant héroïquement à un autre produit des miracles. Tu sais comment Freud s'est révélé à lui-même génie en même temps que poète et grand écrivain ? Par l'identification héroïque à Gœthe ; par la filiation symbolique au

---

38. *Mwambe* is a hearty chicken stew, the national dish of the Democratic Republic of the Congo.

39. In Freudian thought, creativity has to achieve a lift-off, like a bird or airplane taking flight.

génie créateur du grand Gœthe. On connaît l'anecdote. A trente-neuf ans, l'auteur des *Affinités électives*, à l'occasion de son premier voyage à Rome et à Naples, retrouve un renouveau d'inspiration et de style. De même, c'est à trente-neuf ans que Freud se découvre à l'occasion de son premier voyage en Italie. L'identification, la filiation symbolique à un créateur génial est une nécessité.

— Hugo fit de même en s'identifiant à Chateaubriand.[40]

— Oui ! Mais cependant identification n'est pas imitation.

— Mais, est-ce possible de culture à culture ? Entre génies appartenant à des cultures différentes ? Un génie africain peut-il s'identifier symboliquement à un génie européen ?

— Mettrais-tu en doute par hasard et pour la première fois ma culture humaniste qui m'affilie aux Grands Européens ? Ta question vaut cependant la peine d'être posée. Mais pour dissiper toute incertitude, mes dispositions sont prises. Ce qui pourrait enchaîner ma filiation européenne est, à l'instant où je te parle complètement neutralisé. Libérer mon génie, libérer le discours européen enchaîné en moi, c'est identique. Ce n'est plus qu'une

---

40. At age fourteen, the future novelist Victor Hugo vowed to become "Chateaubriand ou rien" (Hugo 297).

question de « décollage ». Icare doit toujours ses ailes à quelque Dédale.

— Maître, comment osez-vous penser pareille chose de Niaiseux ? Ne savez-vous pas que je voue à votre personne un culte inconditionnel ? Tous dans l'Institut devraient agir autant. Si le soleil luit aujourd'hui, c'est grâce à vous.

— Je ne te reproche rien, Niaiseux. Ta question est pertinente. Même les génies ont de temps en temps besoin de dialogue pour affiner leur pensée. Je puis t'annoncer que je « décolle » aujourd'hui, tel le jeune Bergotte de Marcel Proust.[41] « Pour se promener dans les airs, il n'est pas nécessaire d'avoir l'automobile la plus puissante ; mais une automobile qui, ne continuant pas de courir à terre et coupant d'une verticale la ligne qu'elle suivait, soit capable de convertir en force ascensionnelle sa vitesse horizontale. De même ceux qui produisent des œuvres géniales ne sont pas ceux qui, vivant dans le milieu le plus délicat, ont la conversation la plus brillante, la culture la plus étendue, mais ceux qui ont eu le pouvoir, cessant brusquement de vivre pour eux-mêmes, de rendre leur personnalité pareille à un miroir, de telle sorte que leur vie, si médiocre d'ailleurs qu'elle pouvait

41. Bergotte is a great but unappreciated writer in Proust's *À la recherche du temps perdu*, here described in the second volume, *À l'ombre des jeunes filles en fleurs* (554–55).

être mondainement et même, dans un certain sens, intellectuellement parlant, s'y reflète, le génie consistant dans le pouvoir réfléchissant et non dans la qualité intrinsèque du spectacle reflété. Le jour où le jeune Bergotte put montrer au monde de ses lecteurs le salon de mauvais goût où il avait passé son enfance et les causeries très drôles qu'il y tenait avec ses frères, ce jourlà, il monta plus haut que les amis de sa famille, plus spirituels et plus distingués : ceux-ci dans leurs belles Rolls-Royce pourraient rentrer chez eux en témoignant un peu de mépris pour la vulgarité des Bergotte ; mais lui, de son modeste appareil qui venait enfin de "décoller", il les survolait. »

Génial Proust ! Il a raison. Je suis aujourd'hui à ce miroir. Je m'y reflète. Ma créativité n'a jamais été aussi prête à prendre les ailes d'Icare qu'en ce moment. Ce que j'appelle paralysie n'est qu'une incubation. Une longue incubation ! La clé du mystère enfin trouvée ! Je déguste le succès. J'en suis grisé. Des milliers de lecteurs qui tournent tel un essaim d'abeilles. Qui agressent mon texte. Mon œuvre. Compréhensible et incompréhensible. Débordant de sens. Chaque abeille y met son sens. Y suce son suc. Plénitude. Je suis inépuisable. Mon nom voguant à travers l'univers. Étudié, discuté. Objet de mémoires et de thèses. Interviewé à la télévision. Sollicité pour des autographes. Cité dans toutes les anthologies à côté d'autres génies. Dialoguant avec d'autres génies. Idole de la jeunesse. Dans toutes les conversations intellectuelles.

— Maître, vos deux premiers essais et vos recueils de poésie vous classent déjà parmi les classiques les plus célèbres du monde.

— Essayiste. Pas assez. Essayiste, romancier, poète, oui ! Je puis enfin me compter parmi les génies polyvalents. Le Napoléon des lettres africaines. Du monde tout court. Éclat. Brio. Poésie noire. Non, poésie humaine. Je n'ai du Noir que la peau. Mon œuvre me consacre pour l'immortalité. Immortalité laurée ? Non, semence d'immortalité. Malraux crée le surmonde de l'art pour échapper au néant ; une image assez puissante pour réduire le néant à néant. Mon monument — chef-d'œuvre unique — est par lui-même immortalité. Beaucoup de génies, de faux génies à vrai dire, se préoccupent de la survie de leur œuvre. Le vrai génie n'a pas d'inquiétude car il est déjà présence éternelle dans le monde : semence d'immortalité.

— Ces paroles sont tellement inédites, Maître, que je crains qu'elles ne se perdent. Il faudrait un Platon pour les reproduire. Socrate mort, se survit à lui-même. Les vôtres s'envolent. *Verba volant.* Le téléphone supprime toute distance, anéantit l'espace, mais n'enregistre pas vos paroles. J'ai une mémoire trop courte… Il y a des techniciens ingénieux pour nous installer un téléphone combiné qui enregistrerait automatiquement vos paroles.

— Mes paroles échappent, grâce au téléphone, à l'espace. En les fixant sur bandes magnétiques, tu les resoumets à la loi de l'espace. Si l'être humain ne peut y échapper, le génie doit être assez avisé pour trouver un substitut qui lui permette de le maîtriser ; créer une façon de lutter contre l'espace. De même que la littérature gestuelle doit nous révéler à nous-mêmes, ainsi le téléphone par son action nous fait découvrir notre capacité à relever tout défi.

— Votre génie défie toute proposition et toute objection.

— Mon cher Niaiseux, je suis à la croisée des chemins. Je vois mon œuvre exposée au public ; détachée définitivement de moi. Le génie, vois-tu, a ses moments d'angoisse, tel le Christ au Jardin de Gethsémani. Il voit l'œuvre affronter les réactions, les jugements et les critiques. Ou ce qui est plus grave, l'indifférence du public. Le génie méconnu, ça existe ! Soit que l'époque n'est pas suffisamment préparée à l'accueillir soit que, compris, on le refuse.

— Mais tel n'est pas votre cas. Vous êtes au-delà de la reconnaissance par le public.

— Je sacrifie à l'autel de la création. Tu ne sais pas ce que ça me coûte. La solitude. Seul dans cette aventure.

Écartèlement. Déchirement. Comme dans toute parturition. Connais-tu l'angoisse de la mère avant l'enfantement ? La nôtre, incertitude sur la faillite possible de la beauté. Les chemins de la création sont glissants. Des pièges peuvent enchaîner l'écriture. En faire une ombre. En tournant la dernière page de leur œuvre, que de génies ne chantent pas le beau poème de Desnos :

J'ai rêvé tellement de toi
J'ai tellement marché, tellement parlé,
Tellement aimé ton ombre
Qu'il ne reste plus rien de toi.
Il me reste d'être l'ombre parmi les ombres
D'être cent fois plus ombre que l'ombre
D'être l'ombre qui viendra et reviendra dans ta vie
ensommeillée.[42]

Telle est notre condition, mon cher Niaiseux… Livrés au fatum de la création… L'autre ligne retentit. C'est Castino Paqua au bout du fil ! Je me trouve avec deux appareils, l'un à l'oreille gauche, l'autre à l'oreille droite. Me voilà au milieu comme un arbitre de match. Plutôt comme un réconciliateur.

Castino Paqua est aussi une de ces créatures qui me vouent un culte plus calculé que réel. Elle croît à ma

---

42. The concluding lines of "J'ai tant revé de toi" (Desnos 85), said to be the last poem by the French surrealist Robert Desnos (1900–45).

puissance ; que je peux tout arranger pour les Coopérants. Caractère plus léger, plus espiègle, parfaitement déluré. Elle lit beaucoup. Très imprégnée des idées bues dans *Emmanuelle*,[43] elle croit avoir une vocation. Ayant sacrifié à l'autel de Mario, elle veut être la missionnaire de la bonne nouvelle qui doit révolutionner l'amour traditionnel et apprendre les pièges de l'amour-sentiment.

Elle me téléphone pour me mettre au courant des dernières excroissances des rumeurs locales.

— Es-tu au courant de ce qu'on propage sur toi ?

— Encore ?

— Oui, bien sûr ! Le jour où il n'y aura plus de rumeur, ce sera la fin de tout. Plus de respiration. Plus de regard. Plus de clins d'œil. Plus de reniflement. Déjà le paradis !

— J'ai hâte d'apprendre…

— Maître, le poème de Desnos est d'une beauté exquise. Pourriez-vous me le répéter. J'ai le crayon tout près pour le noter.

— Tu peux le trouver dans le recueil des poèmes de Desnos à la page deux cent cinquante.

— On raconte qu'on te voit à la messe des catholiques. L'Althussérien, l'homme de gauche sacrifie maintenant à

43. An erotic novel (1967) by Emmanuelle Arsan, in which the avid Emmanuelle is instructed in free love by Mario, an aging gay voyeur.

l'autel YANKEE ! Fait la cour aux capitalistes... L'humanisme du refus!...

— Tu es bouleversée ? Tout cela s'accommode des intérêts du moment à défendre. La tactique, voilà une chose que tu dois encore apprendre.

— Il me semble que Desnos frappe de nullité l'œuvre antérieure ?

— C'est pourquoi l'écriture devrait être un lieu montreur d'ombres. Paradoxe ? Non. Ombres de ce qu'elle n'est pas.

— Mais tous ne le comprennent pas ainsi. Beaucoup te lâchent. Opportunisme et défense réelle des intérêts se confondent.

Elle raccroche. J'essaie de la rappeler. Le téléphone sonne. Mais elle devine que c'est moi qui veux la rattraper. Je coupe. Mon génie n'est pas de ceux-là qui se laissent impressionner par les dires d'une fille. Du reste le seul bien que j'en retire est encore un avantage pour elle. Une information de temps en temps. A ne pas négliger. Tout fait nombre.

Je coupe aussi l'autre ligne. Niaiseux se perdant dans des exclamations de plus en plus béates.

Au dehors la chute du soleil ne progresse pas. Un vent frais me bat de plein fouet le visage. Je referme la fenêtre.

J'ai toujours peur d'une rechute de bronchite. Faible de santé, les moindres imprudences me coûtent cher. Je me remets d'ailleurs d'une maladie qui a failli m'enlever la vie. Le médecin dit : « Plus d'alcool. Plus de cigarette. Plus de… ». Mais c'est mon suicide ! Il envisage un traitement à l'étranger. Un départ ! Ce serait un retard considérable pour mes travaux. Par ailleurs, il y a un avantage : les contacts avec des collègues étrangers. Ceux qui me connaissent. Ceux qui ne me connaissent pas. Élargir le diamètre du cercle de ma réputation. Glisser par-ci par-là mes cartes de visite. Mon état bio-bibliographique déjà surchargé. Mes recherches cataloguées : 1. Livres. 2. Ouvrages collectifs. 3. Ouvrages sous presse. 4. Ouvrages achevés non encore déposés.[44] 5. Ouvrages achevés en voie d'être déposés. 6. Ouvrages en voie d'achèvement. 7. Ouvrages en chantier. 8. Ouvrages simplement conçus. 9. Ouvrages préconçus. 10. Ouvrages en voie de décollage. 11. Ouvrages simplement mus par la force pulsionnelle. 12. Ouvrages en voie d'être livrés. 13. Articles. 14. Articles en collaboration. 15. Articles terminés et déposés. 16. Articles terminés non encore déposés. 17. Articles sous presse. 18. Articles simplement conçus. 19. Articles mijotés. 20. Articles de création. 21. Articles

44. A copy of every book published in France has to be sent to the Bibliothèque Nationale de France.

scientifiques. 22. Articles de sociologie. 23. Articles de critique littéraire. 24. Articles divers… Quel talent polyvalent ? Quel talent pluridimensionnel ? Je lis des réactions sur tous les visages quand je passe. « Il écrit avec autant d'aisance sur la critique littéraire ; sur l'économie ; sur l'anthropologie ; sur la théologie ; sur la linguistique, sur la graphologie. » Je vois les hommes s'écarter sur mon passage et courber leur tête en signe de vénération. « Le savant passe. Il ne parle pas beaucoup. Il est sententieux. Sec, sobre dans ses paroles. Tête légèrement inclinée. Les cheveux pas trop bien peignés. »

Mes écrits impressionnent. La clé ? Les références. L'*Encyclopedia Britannica* produit ses effets. Le procédé utilisé génial. Des ouvrages cités mais jamais lus. Les comptes rendus de la revue *Culture et développement*, instrument précieux de la mystification !

— Allô !

— Niaiseux au bout du fil !

— Ah ! Tu téléphones à propos ! Une idée intéressante. Nous avons à l'Institut des Chinois, des Japonais. Que penses-tu si je faisais traduire mes derniers essais et les publier sans la mention « Traduit en chinois par Sing chiang Chu » et « Traduit en japonais par Hitachi Huyafusia yama » ? Signés par contre « GIAMBATISTA VIKO » ? L'impression produite sur le public serait évidente. L'auteur connaît ces deux langues. Qu'en penses-tu ?

— L'idée me paraît alléchante. D'autres l'ont déjà tentée avec succès. Déontologiquement parlant, ce n'est pas de la malhonnêteté intellectuelle. Vous profitez simplement des services rendus par autrui !

— Aucun savant aujourd'hui ne peut se passer de la connaissance de plusieurs langues internationales. Connaître l'anglais — je ne parle pas du français, la chose va de soi — l'espagnol, le russe, c'est bien. Le japonais, c'est encore mieux ; le chinois c'est encore dix fois mieux car l'avenir, la clé de l'avenir, appartient à l'Asie, plus particulièrement à la Chine. Les Occidentaux ont terriblement peur du péril jaune. Mais combien de temps peuvent-ils prétendre tenir le coup. Ils savent lutter contre la fièvre jaune, la juguler. Mais contre le péril jaune, ils ne peuvent rien.

Des traductions ! Ça allongera la liste de mes publications. Une seule fausse note : le roman piétine. Les quelques lignes déjà écrites ne semblent pas honorer mon génie. Un style au croisement de plusieurs tendances contradictoires : l'incantatoire, le doctoral, le pathétique, l'oraculaire. Tantôt fulgurant ; éclatant ; tantôt déconstruit ; tantôt des brusques opacités, tantôt des profondes transparences. Discours interne de l'obsessionnel dilué dans un mélange indescriptible de temps et de confusion de perspectives. La ponctuation ? N'en dis rien. L'échec semble poindre à l'horizon.

— Maître, on ne devrait jamais entendre ce mot de votre bouche. J'y vois plutôt un signe de génie. Une manière de sortir de l'académisme desséchant du roman africain.

— Peut-être ! Des tendances contradictoires dans un même texte ne concourent-elles pas à l'annihilation de celui-ci ? A la célébration de ses pompes funèbres ? Mais une chose m'inquiète : une cohabitation très troublante d'éléments hétéroclites.

— Vous ne faites que vous plaindre. Mais n'y aurait-il pas lieu de se laisser initier pour accéder à la science de l'écriture ?

— C'est aussi une idée ! L'initié est un autre. Il est celui qui est passé de l'ignorance à la science, au vrai savoir. La *scienza nuova* que je cherche. Notre culture, je veux dire — l'occidentale — n'a plus le sens de l'initiation. Plus personne n'y croit. Seul l'Occident se trouve dans cette situation. Partout ailleurs elle existe. Crois-tu qu'un Occidental qui irait dans une société étrangère pour se laisser initier accéderait réellement à la science ? La nouvelle science serait en fait un autre état de conscience qui informerait les rapports avec les êtres et les choses. Mais la réalisation ne conduit-elle pas à l'accomplissement personnel ? L'Occidental, incroyant, serait-il capable d'une telle métamorphose ? Comment pourrait-il prétendre accéder à cet état de grâce ?

— Les choses étant ainsi présentées, ce geste ne serait qu'une mascarade.

— Impossibilité donc d'accéder à cet autre « Je » ! Car l'initiation est un passage de la nature à la culture. L'équation passage de l'ignorance à la science = passage de la nature à la culture. Ailleurs qu'en Occident, l'initié arrive à l'être ; à la découverte du sens profond des choses ; à lire au-delà du sensible ; à comprendre les liens cosmiques de l'existence humaine et la dimension intérieure de l'homme.

— L'initiation n'opère qu'à l'intérieur de la même culture.

Les ethnologues qui en trompant à coup de sel, d'argent, ces tribus d'Afrique ou de l'Amazonie, violent leur altérité, commettent un acte sacrilège qui les conduit finalement à la folie.

— C'est cette contradiction au cœur de ce geste sacrilège qui empêche la réalisation personnelle.

— Mais cela ne devrait pas vous rebuter, Maître. La vie n'est-elle pas une contradiction ? Tiens, voilà une masse d'intellectuels en Afrique qui sont coopérants dans leur propre pays et parviennent à se bâtir une bonne situation. L'analogie n'est pas, bien sûr, identité. Mais elle est éclairante.

— Quand il s'agit d'une société désacralisée, la contradiction peut conduire à la réalisation personnelle. Mais quelle réalisation personnelle ? Matérielle, oui ! Ceci ne conduit pas plus loin que cela. C'est ce que nous voyons chez bon nombre d'intellectuels en Occident. J'en suis très inquiet. Car tous les intellectuels sont un peu dans ce même cas...

Moment de silence entre Niaiseux et moi... Je crois reconnaître comme en rêve l'écho menaçant de certaines paroles :

> Ceux qui t'arrachent à notre univers
> Ceux qui t'introduisent dans l'univers de
> Ceux qui chaque jour nous tuent à petit feu
> Ceux qui paralysent nos énergies au bénéfice des
> étrangers meurent à jamais par ce sang
> que tu bois.
> Malheur à quiconque ose recourir à nous pour
> servir des intérêts étrangers !
> A bon entendeur salut !

— Maître, le problème me paraît d'une extrême gravité : dépasser la simple contradiction classique surmontée dans la synthèse de la thèse et de l'antithèse. La coexistence des cultures différentes dans un individu est une source constante de déchirement.

On n'est plus « un » mais « deux », « trois », « hétérogène ». Si vous vous lancez dans l'écriture, ce sera le discours de « deux, de « trois ». Un texte hétérogène. Des morceaux. Détachés. Sans lien. Plusieurs parlent à la fois. Le texte apparaît plutôt comme une matrice à produire des éléments de promiscuité. Les mouvements des phrases donnent des effets surprenants. Des mots d'halluciné. Des fantasmes. Des coins d'ombres. Un feu d'artifice. Fulgurance. Rhétorique. Effet chorégraphique. Sonore. Gluant. Agglutiné. Agglutinant. Graphie musicale. Rythmique. Partouzes verbales. Le décollage est obtenu. Mais le résultat ? Le voilà.

— Il y a, en effet, en moi plusieurs discours. Aucun d'eux n'est parfaitement maîtrisé. Signe de déchirement en dépit de mon choix. Plusieurs semblent parler à la fois. On ne renie peut-être pas sa mère impunément. Au propre comme au figuré. Tel est mon cas. Sais-tu que les miens m'appellent « un Blanc ». Nous n'avons plus de commun que la peau. Sur le plan culturel, un abîme infranchissable nous sépare. Seule la solidarité biologique nous lie encore. Mais qu'est-ce que le biologique au regard du culturel ? Il faudrait nous rencontrer dans la nature. Un retour pour moi à la nature. Une démarche contre-culturelle. Mais le réenracinement est-il possible ? Et comment ? L'Afrique s'est déracinée en moi. On l'a tuée dans l'œuf. L'Occident s'y est planté. Y a-t-il possibilité de jeter le pont entre les deux patries ?

— Les poètes par la magie du verbe y parviennent. Mais ils restent tiraillés par un ailleurs. C'est ça qui les définit. Si celui-ci disparaissait, il n'y aurait plus de tension ; plus de poésie. Jean Amrouche éternellement tiraillé entre l'amont et l'aval.[45] L'amont : les ancêtres fabuleux. L'aval : le présent, l'avenir. Il voulait être à la fois les deux. Il cherchait son nom. « Mon nom est Homme. Je le sais, mais l'Homme est toujours un homme, cet homme que je suis.

Pour l'instant, j'ai le sentiment d'être condamné à la différence, à une irréductible et inquiétante singularité... Le champ de bataille est en moi : nulle parcelle de mon esprit et de mon âme qui n'appartienne à la fois aux deux camps qui s'entretuent. Je suis algérien, je crois être pleinement français. » Nous sommes un champ de bataille. L'écriture en est le lieu d'expression.

— Oui, lieu de réconciliation avec nous-mêmes. Lieu de détente momentanée. Car la quête reste jamais assouvie parce que la bataille jamais éteinte. Le style toujours soumis à la torture : notre nom propre et notre identité.

— Le choix est-il encore possible ?

— Illusoire.

— Comme tout dans la vie. Mais illusoirement apaisant.

---

45. Jean Amrouche was a francophone Algerian poet (1906–62). His *Journal, 1928–1962* has entries that resonate with Viko's preoccupations: "Je ne suis pas de la race de ceux qui font carrière. Mes frères sont Nerval et Rimbaud" (77). "Devenir français . . . est toujours à imiter. . . . Au final, c'est se condamner à ne pas être" (315).

Ces derniers mots de Niaiseux tombent comme un voile sur mon esprit. La nuit approche. Les derniers rayons du soleil donnent encore une pâleur à l'horizon. La lutte entre le jour et la nuit semble être gagnée par celle-ci. Lutte de l'Ange et de l'Homme.

III

Assis à ma table. Rideaux des fenêtres tirés. Je contemple les poules qui s'entêtent à ne pas vouloir regagner le poulailler. Un coq domine. Seul mâle au milieu de la vingtaine que compte tout mon pensionnat, il semble avoir aussi une mission spéciale. Les poules, en cercle, s'approchent. S'en écartent. Lui, monte l'une, l'autre. Geste mythique. Rituel. En apparence libre. Mais hors du temps. Éternel. Présent dans l'intensité du présent. Évanescence dans le présent. Réglé par aucune loi. Je pense à Castino Paqua. Ne devrait-elle pas observer « scientifiquement » ces créatures ; prendre exemple sur elles ? Le coq aborde ses terrains sans préjugé, sans appréhension, avec l'espoir d'y trouver de nouvelles raisons d'intérêt, et avec le souci de réussir. Mais ne suis-je pas injuste de prêter à la pauvre fille de telles idées ? Sa chère Emmanuelle dit : la liberté est le contraire de l'ignorance. Or cette colonie devant moi est un royaume d'ignorants…

— Allô, ici Climax !

— Salut, vieux sauvage. Comment vas-tu ? Sirbu est parmi nous. Quelle chance pour l'Institut !

— Oui, je crois, c'est une chance. Il faudra l'exploiter à fond. C'est un gars qui a beaucoup d'idées. Il faut savoir s'en servir.

— Des dispositions sont prises. Je maîtrise mal l'allemand. Je pense lui confier la traduction de plusieurs de mes articles et essais.

— Excellente idée ! Je pourrais me charger du portugais. Qu'en penses-tu ?

— Parfait. J'estime fort à sa juste valeur ce genre de collaboration. Avec vous autres, elle est possible. Mais avec les Nègres!…

— C'est ce que, tous, nous constatons. Il n'y en a pas deux dans tout le pays de votre trempe. Ils parlent beaucoup, ils veulent avoir des grands postes.

— Les Nègres sont fils de la déesse Jalousie. Moi, je ne tiens pas à continuer à œuvrer parmi eux. Fonctionnaire français de par mes activités culturelles et scientifiques, je rêve de ce jour où je me retrouverai à Paris. Tout en moi est un appel, tel Lucien de Rubempré,[46] vers Paris. Comprends-tu tout mon martyr ? Votre présence est pour moi un soulagement.

— Je crains que notre départ ne soit une catastrophe !

— Tu es un des rares qui comprennes ma situation ; le fantasme qui nuit et jour me poursuit. La singularité de mon expérience traduit le malaise qui ronge tel un cancer ma vie.

---

46. A protagonist in Balzac's *La comédie humaine* who comes from the provinces to conquer Parisian society.

— On te comprend d'instinct. Ton discours est le nôtre. Miroir de l'Occident qui s'y reconnaît.

— Tu es un vrai poète, Climax !

— Nous vous donnons toutes les chances, à toi et à tes collègues africains, d'apprendre à accoucher de ce discours. Certains veulent lui opposer un hypothétique discours africain, érigé en entreprise de déréification du regard ethnocentrique de l'Occident. Grossière aberration. Tentative vouée à l'échec dans l'œuf. Le peuventils ? Sur quelle base prendre appui ? Nous vous avons tout donné y compris la possibilité de nous contester.

— Climax, je t'en prie!...

— Quand je dis vous, tu n'es pas compris dans ce pronom, à vrai dire ambigu. Je m'indigne et m'élève contre cette prétention de vouloir ériger aujourd'hui les mythes, les légendes, les contes africains en discours scientifiques. On nous combat en brandissant un système de croyances immuables ; en nous opposant une africanité ou une personnalité africaine hypothétique. Pamphlets, manifestes, essais inondent le marché. Notre magnanimité ouvre largement nos maisons d'édition à ces fadaises où l'Occident est traîné dans la boue ; insulté, piétiné. Notre dire remis en question avec une désinvolture inqualifiable attend la relève par une pratique scientifique proprement africaine ? La nouvelle idéologie est une contre-idéologie. Mais on oublie que la science n'est pas fille de l'idéologie.

— Ta rhétorique est d'une violence à renverser les montagnes. Les Africains pourraient te rétorquer : le besoin fort ressenti chez vous d'ensauvager la vie que dessèche votre hyper-science est né du contact avec l'Afrique. Vous parquez l'homme dans des réserves conceptuelles ruineuses : essence ; existence ; raison ; etc. L'homme a besoin d'être décolonisé et colonisé en Occident. La décolonisation vous l'apprendrez chez nous ; la colonisation, l'Afrique vous l'offre généreusement. L'homme exfolié de sa richesse la retrouvera dans le continent resté vierge.

— J'admets que nous tendons aux Africains une arme miraculeuse par l'emploi incontrôlé et abusif d'un vocabulaire mal défini.[47] Les métaphores ne doivent jamais masquer la vérité. Elles exhalent trop de parfums romantiques et rousseauistes.

— En somme, c'est un piège. Et les Occidentaux et les Africains y succombent sans s'en rendre compte. Les premiers confondent genre littéraire et réalité ; les seconds s'y sentent à l'aise comme dans leur élément naturel. Le mythe de l'ensauvagement vient ainsi renforcer leur

47. Alluding to Césaire's surrealist poem *Les armes miraculeuses* (*Complete Poetry* 62–305), which features strings of disconnected phrases, "les enfantillages de l'alphabet des spasmes" from "la berceuse congolaise que les soudards m'ont désapprise" (106).

adhésion à un univers d'imbrication du profane et du sacré, de vision totalisante. Mais une chose m'inquiète. Malgré le rouleau compresseur de la colonisation, de la science et de la technique occidentales, les voix africaines ont encore aujourd'hui beaucoup plus de puissance pour nourrir nos rêves, nos passions.

Chargées d'une présence obsédante elles ébranlent même les esprits les plus lucides de notre temps. Fautil rayer d'un trait de plume ces personnages des mythes, des légendes, leurs cris, leurs pleurs et leurs rires qui pour l'homme moderne sont comme une enfance retrouvée. Ils viennent nous tirer de notre solitude, nous mettent dans un réseau d'échange, de communication avec l'univers.

— J'y accorde un regard méthodologique qui nous apprend à regarder l'autre avec un brin d'amour.

— Tu crois à un échange entre civilisations ?

— Au niveau méthodologique, oui.

— Mais comment concevoir une efficacité méthodologique sans une réelle célébration du monde à travers les mêmes gammes d'harmonies que l'Afrique ? Celleci reste, dans cette logique, dans ta logique, ce pur objet qui doit servir tes intérêts. L'amour a-t-il encore placé dans l'asservissement ?

— Tu m'accules à dire que tout n'est finalement qu'intérêt égoïste y compris notre propre regard sur nous-mêmes. L'amour est au paradis des mythes ; il n'est qu'ombre ici-bas.

— Mais quelle est la limite entre l'ombre et la réalité ? Est bien malin qui peut te la donner. Quelle est la limite entre la vie et la mort ; entre ce qui est « sapiens », et « demens » en nous ? Entre le normal et l'anormal ? L'ombre commence où se termine la réalité ; la mort où se termine la vie ; le « sapiens », le normal où commencent le « demens » et l'anormal.

— C'est dire que l'amour commence où finit l'intérêt égoïste.

Je raccroche. Des discussions avec mes amis nous placent hors du temps. Nous restons accrochés au téléphone sans nous rendre compte que le temps s'écoule, servis par une complicité étonnante du coucher du soleil. Toutes les lignes simultanément occupées m'installent au milieu de la scène de théâtre dont je suis le meneur de jeu ; le centre vers où tout converge ; cerveau noyau ressemblant à cet espace-temps primordial dont je rêve la traduction dans mon roman. Chacun de mes amis est comme un atome gravitant autour de moi. J'arrête le temps. J'annihile l'espace. Moi. Une horloge qui tourne sans que les heures du jour défilent. Un train en marche sans brûler les espaces. Ma maison, cette matrice primordiale rêvée. On ne s'y rend pas. On y est présent. Il n'est pas cinq heures ; six heures. Non. Le temps est immobile. Je suis le temps. Je suis l'espace. Temps vaincu, sur tes décombres j'élève des rythmes purs ! Danse folle. Espace gratte-ciel de la durée. Archipel du bonheur. De la science. Bonheur et science : deux frère et sœur. Havre. Fontaine de jouvence. Plaisirs enchantés.

IV

La porte s'ouvre.

— Tu as la tête enfoncée dans les bras !

— Oh ! chérie ! La parturition tarde à venir. L'intuition est là. Éblouissante. Chance singulière. Il faut lui donner forme. Je connais les ressources physiques, les désirs, le caractère de mon héroïne. Je la vois devant moi, éblouissante de couleurs et de vie. Je voudrais que tu la voies aussi dans l'éclairage de sa beauté, de son intelligence. Ouvre tes yeux. Regarde. Elle sort de l'invisible vision. Je voudrais que l'écriture la secoue ; la bouscule, la sorte de la fiction ; lui donne vie. Qu'elle cesse d'être simple comparse de mes songes. Écoute. Elle me parle, te parle lui parle. Alerte, vive, besogneuse.

Coiffée. Parfumée. Parée pour la cérémonie…

— Quelle cérémonie ?

— Une réception sans doute ?

— Que dit-elle ?

— Rien !

— Quels souliers porte-t-elle ?

— Hauts talons, brun-beige !

— Est-elle accompagnée par quelqu'un ?

— Par son mari sans doute ! Celui-ci semble très jaloux. Il ne la quitte pas une seconde. Les voilà à la réception. Dans une ambassade. Le Tout… est présent.[48] On la salue respectueusement. Longuement. Ceci ne semble pas trop plaire à son homme. On se retourne ; on la suit. Soleil resplendissant.

— Ce qui se conçoit bien, s'énonce clairement. Traduit dans l'art : le vécu s'extériorise facilement. Comme on vit, on écrit. Et non : comme on écrit, on vit.

— Ton intuition m'impressionne, me trouble !

— Je ne fais qu'énoncer un truisme. L'écriture, c'est l'homme. Comme on dit, le style, c'est l'homme.[49] On ne peut conduire une écriture parallèlement à sa vie. L'écriture suit l'homme.

— Tel homme, telle écriture. Ce qui ne veut pas dire que l'art imite la vie. Dans un certain sens, oui. Même les œuvres les plus imaginaires, les plus éloignées de notre monde quotidien, sont encore en quelque sorte une certaine imitation. Traduction en clair : la duplicité du cœur, l'insincérité conduit droit à l'échec dans l'art. Beaucoup d'hommes sont portés vers l'écriture par le snobisme, le goût du jour, le vent, l'intérêt. La paralysie dans l'art vient de là. Il s'agit d'être authentique — Oh ! le mot est galvaudé — aussi bien dans la vie que dans l'art. L'écriture

48. Evoking the common expression *le Tout-Paris*.

49. An aphorism from the the Comte de Buffon's 1753 work *Discours sur le style* (18).

ne vient pas occuper une place seconde, juxtaposée à la vie. Elle reçoit son être vrai de la vie. C'est dans ce sens que l'on dit le style, c'est l'homme. Tiens, voilà l'œuvre de Malraux. L'auteur de *La condition humaine* parle de la mort avec une sincérité, livre après livre, grave, exemplaire.[50] Non que Malraux ait connu la mort. Mais il en a une dramatique expérience. Il ne la connaît pas par des livres. Dans les situations rapportées par lui, la mort s'insinue dans son être par l'affrontement de face au temps de la Résistance, par la maladie maintenant. Le seul moyen de continuer à vivre lui paraît l'écriture. C'est pourquoi *La tête d'Obsidienne* ; *Lazare* ; *L'irréel* sont des livres ayant valeur de témoignage.

— On croirait entendre Salomon parler par ta bouche. Tu te meus dans ces notions avec une sagesse, une spontanéité toutes bibliques. Tes paroles tranchent autant par leur justesse que par leur gravité. Je les bois comme une eau apaisante. *In ore infantium sapientia.*[51] La vérité vient des enfants, parce qu'il sont purs. Tes paroles sont pures. Dépouillées. C'est l'artiste qui parle en toi. Tu portes en toi l'espérance de créativité. Tu vois juste.

---

50. André Malraux (1901–76) wrote novels about his early adventures in Indochina and his anti-fascist activities during the Spanish Civil War and World War II, as well as works on the theory of art. His 1933 novel *La condition humaine* concerns a failed Communist rebellion in Shanghai.

51. "Out of the mouths of babes comes wisdom" (Psalm 8.2).

C'est ça la source de l'art. Nous autres les femmes, de par la maternité, nous sommes des artistes. Nos enfants sont des chefs-d'œuvre d'art, parce que nous portons en nous essentiellement l'espérance de la maternité. Une femme qui en manquerait, elle aurait beau immobiliser toutes les ressources de l'intelligence, de l'imagination, et financières, elle n'accéderait pas à ce chef-d'œuvre de la nature qu'est la parturition. L'art est aussi œuvre de parturition.

— Arrivent à produire ceux qui croient d'abord dans l'espérance d'innovation. Ce n'est pas le jugement du public qui fait que l'enfant né ou à naître est œuvre d'art, mais l'espérance. Le public ne fait que constater. Beaucoup de gens restent paralysés par l'idée du jugement du public à affronter. Grave erreur. L'art est — en deçà et au-delà — du public.

— Le public répond donc à une autre notion. Surajoutée : la notion de communication. La création en tant que telle n'appelle pas le public quoiqu'en disent certains auteurs.

— Mais les mots sont un univers signifiant !

— Je n'en disconviens pas. C'est une autre dimension, si tu veux, de l'œuvre. Question de priorité logique. Si tu restes rivé au problème de la communication, tu ne pigeras pas un mot. Ton roman n'avancera pas d'un pouce. D'ailleurs pourquoi te préoccuper tant du public.

L'œuvre, une fois lâchée, ne t'appartient plus. Elle est pâture livrée aux pourceaux de la critique. Elle devient une citadelle que l'on prend d'assaut. Ta belle héroïne devant qui tu t'extasies devient chez certains ton double ; chez d'autres, objet de ton aliénation... Un bon nombre la déshabillent, la rhabillent ; la torturent, la cajolent, la prostituent. Tu ne la reconnais plus. C'est çà le public. Indiscrétion. Dénudation. Impudeur. Telles sont les zones dans lesquelles il aime se mouvoir. Devant cette sorte d'iconoclasme masochiste, tu ne reconnais plus ta fille « œuvre ». Le public cisèle à nouveau. Taille dans le marbre à sa manière. Fait le « Striptease » de ton œuvre. Tu te vois alors agressé de toutes parts. Orphelin. Veuf. Mari. Amant. Cocu. Boudé par les uns, haï par les autres.

— Vaut-il encore la peine d'écrire si telle est la condition de l'œuvre et de l'expérience de l'écriture ? C'est tout juste si l'œuvre ne te renie pas.

— L'expérience de l'écriture est semblable à celle de la paternité ou de la maternité. Tu mets au monde aujourd'hui un enfant. Grand, jeune homme, jeune fille, ton enfant peut refuser de te reconnaître. Pourtant que de sueurs, de larmes, pour l'élever ! Nous ne l'élevons pas pour nous, mais pour lui-même. Un proverbe dit : « Tant que tu as la force de procréer, aie le plus d'enfants. Il s'en trouvera un qui te reconnaîtra. » Il en est de même de l'écriture. Produis le plus possible. L'une de tes œuvres fera de toi ce que tu souhaites être. Comment penses-tu intituler ce roman ? La passion de… ne conviendrait-il pas mieux comme titre ?

— Titre trop religieux ! Cela évoquerait la passion du Christ ou de je ne sais quel saint catholique… Le titre doit être évocateur. En rapport avec le dessein central de mes recherches. Un autre personnage historique pourrait faire l'affaire.

— Mais pour l'instant, le titre paraît secondaire. L'essentiel est que tu « décolles ».

Pendant qu'elle me parle, mes yeux tombent sur une photo encadrée du château de la principauté de Monaco. Souvenir d'une visite en compagnie d'un étudiant gabonais. Édifice illuminé. Rouge. Blanc. Bateau. Drapeaux français plantés, dorés. Posés sur un socle. Assis dans le restaurant attenant à la salle de jeux. Mon compagnon et moi. Devant nous une fille. Seule. Eh ! Lise ! Elle ne fait mie ! Image de l'incommunicabilité des races, des civilisations. Nouvelle interpellation.[52] Nouveau défi.

— Ne crois-tu pas qu'il nous faudrait inventer une littérature qui protège les écrivains contre le public ? Qui fasse participer le public à la rédaction du texte ? Formule

52. In "Idéologie et appareils idéologiques d'état," Louis Althusser argued that a state transforms individuals into subjects by interpellating (hailing) them in social situations.

« Littérature ouverte », comme cela existe pour la TV « ouverte » à la BBC.

Donner la parole au public, lui permettre de faire de la littérature « Community Programs » (Programmes du public). N'importe qui pourrait donner à l'écrivain une idée et, surtout, la formule exacte. La dichotomie auteur-public disparaîtrait. Il n'y aurait plus de censeur d'un côté, d'écrivain de l'autre. Plus qu'un seul personnage : l'auteur écrivain-public.

— Ce serait une révolution ou une irrévolution copernicienne. « Open Door » donnerait au moins aux gens conscience de la difficulté d'écrire un bon livre.[53]

— Davantage : les rapports entre l'écrivain et ses lecteurs seraient améliorés. La formule créerait un sentiment de participation, de double courant. « Monsieur-tout-le-monde » au lieu d'être receveur d'idées, de valeurs, en serait un créateur. L'idée est géniale. Digne de GIAMBATISTA. Mais pour que personne d'autre ne s'en empare, il faudrait prendre toutes les précautions.

— On commence demain ?

— Demain est un mot proscrit de mon vocabulaire. J'ai pacté avec le présent.

— Prendre un brevet d'invention ?

---

53. This literary initiative parodies the Open Door policy promulgated by the United States to support free trade with China and to uphold its territorial integrity against foreign occupation.

— Cela retarderait l'exécution du projet.

— Tout de suite alors !

— Bien sûr !

— Monsieur, vous me connaissez ?

— Non, pas du tout !

— Vraiment ?

— Je crois que vous déraillez, Monsieur !

— Madame, connaissez-vous GIAMBATISTA ?

— Qu'est-ce que c'est, un animal ?

— Non, c'est un homme.

— Alors, je regrette beaucoup, Monsieur !

— Mademoiselle ! Mademoiselle !

— Je suis pressée, Monsieur !

Elle met peut-être en doute mes bonnes intentions !

— Chérie, c'est une vraie surprise, voire même un SCANDALE.

La rue semble ignorer le professeur GIAMBATISTA !

— Ce sont peut-être des étrangers !

— Non, c'est un scandale ! Qui ne me connaît pas dans ce pays ? Je vois la nécessité de rédiger nous-mêmes des interviews et de les confier à tous les journaux de la place.

— Tu sais bien, chéri, que je réprouve de tels procédés. Cela nous déshonore !

— L'honneur tel que tu l'entends est fort traditionnel. Dépassé. Petit-bourgeois. Du conservatisme larvé. Du conformisme. De la morale établie. Des idées reçues. Toutes faites. Qu'est-ce que l'honneur quand il s'agit d'asseoir ma réputation ? Dans le monde international, elle est faite ; seules quelques garces de ce pays ne me connaissent pas. C'est intolérable. Analphabétisme. Sous-développement ou plutôt sous-équipement intellectuel. Des maux incurables.

— Recommençons l'expérience, chéri ! Je t'en prie. Elle peut être fructueuse.

— Il faut trouver d'autres formules. Plus accessibles à leur captum. Il se peut aussi que le vocabulaire utilisé par moi soit un peu rébarbatif. Déformation professionnelle à laquelle je peux remédier facilement.

— Monsieur, le professeur Giambatista vient de mettre au point un nouveau style appelé à révolutionner l'expérience de l'écriture. Style de « Open Door » (porte ouverte). Seriez-vous d'accord pour participer à cette révolution démocratique ? Révolution démocratique, en effet. Jusqu'à présent, l'écriture est une entreprise bourgeoise qui consiste à transmettre dans un livre des idées toutes faites, établies ; un système de valeurs que vous subissez ; que vous recevez passivement sans que vous preniez part à sa création. « Open Door » remet tout cela en cause. Démocratise l'écriture. C'est vous qui écrivez vous-même le livre. Celui-ci n'est plus une émanation bourgeoise mais votre propre création. Finie la création aliénante, bourgeoise !

— Parfaitement d'accord, Monsieur !

— Quelques précautions, cependant, Monsieur ! « Open Door » admet toutes les idées, sauf les conservatrices ; les toutes faites... vous comprenez !

— Bien sûr !

— Allez-y !

— Le monde est arrivé à un point tel que des fous arrêtent impunément tout passant. Le questionnent. Le...

— Arrête. Les fous ! Vous vous moquez de moi, Monsieur !

Je tente l'expérience avec un autre passant.

« Enfin, c'est le grand jour. Cela me rappelle une chanson que l'on nous faisait brailler quand on avait encore l'âge de porter des culottes courtes. La journée promet d'être belle. Il fait très chaud, et j'ai hâte de me retrouver dans la fraîcheur de la nature et de laisser tomber mes vêtements afin de pouvoir prendre un peu de soleil... »

— Merci, Monsieur. Cela fait l'impression d'une leçon apprise par cœur. Du reste ça manque de consistance et ne nous mène guère très loin. Au revoir Monsieur !

Tentons avec un troisième.

« J'aime bien découvrir au hasard des promenades, les coins pittoresques d'une ville. Je suis déjà venu dans ce coin, mais jamais, je n'ai profité de l'occasion pour me balader lentement dans les rues, pour le simple plaisir de la découvrir. Aujourd'hui j'ai tout mon temps, je vais donc en profiter. Mais la joie de découvrir enfin cette ville, ne me fait pas oublier de jeter des coups d'œil d'admiration sur un tas de belles femmes que je croise dans la rue. Je suis vraiment conquis par le charme de cette ville. On ne se sent pas tellement dépaysé, car la ville a un petit côté cosmopolite, qui ressemble beaucoup à Montréal.

En fait, je crois bien que Sherbrooke ressemble beaucoup plus à Montréal que Québec.[54] Québec est une ville très spéciale, elle est avant tout une ville très française. Ici, il y a beaucoup d'Anglais. »

— Monsieur, je crois que ce début est plaisant et constitue un cadre pour un roman !

— Oui, je pourrais en tirer un cadre de roman dont l'action se passerait au Québec.

Un quatrième :

« Il est près de quatre heures, quand enfin je me décide à abandonner mon lit duveteux et douillet. Je passe à la salle de bain afin de faire ma toilette et ensuite, je fonce sur le réfrigérateur, afin de me préparer un plantureux

---

54. Sherbrooke is the small city in southern Quebec where Georges Ngal began writing his novel.

repas. J'ai une faim de loup. Les exercices ça creuse l'appétit et aussi il y a l'air frais et sain de la campagne. Je me prépare donc un bon gros steak bien cuit avec de bonnes pommes de terre cuites au four. Un véritable festin, que je déguste bien lentement, tout en buvant un couple de bonnes bouteilles de bière.

Le reste de la journée et de la soirée, se passe très calmement, je reste assis sur ma galerie, à écouter les bruits de la nature et à regarder le ciel étoilé. C'est terrible le nombre d'étoiles, que l'on peut voir dans le ciel. Ça fait un bon bout de temps que je n'avais pas eu l'occasion de passer une soirée à regarder le ciel. Une fois de temps à autre, c'est une activité qui a certains charmes. »

— Vous pouvez disposer, Monsieur !

— Ce n'est pas avec de tels morceaux que tu arriveras à révolutionner l'expérience de l'écriture. A l'irrévolution peut-être !

— L'expérience ne semble pas concluante. Si les masses sont indispensables pour opérer les révolutions politiques, elles semblent plutôt inaptes aux révolutions littéraires. Source d'inertie. Pour qu'elles bougent, le souffle doit leur être insufflé d'ailleurs.

Il y a un mot que je n'ose prononcer. Qui ne peut surgir de ma bouche. Interdit. Tabou. Déshonneur. Indignité. Celui d'échec. Mon génie, l'imaginer, le frôler, le caresser, ne peut. Je le hais.

Traître, tu ne peux figurer dans les dictionnaires. Banni à jamais de la francophonie ; du royaume des Lettres. Maudite soit la bouche qui te profère. Maudit l'esprit qui se l'imagine. Maudits les yeux qui te voient. Maudites les oreilles qui t'entendent proférer d'une bouche maudite elle-même. Maudites les narines qui te reniflent. Ma haine te dévore. Te triture très traîtreusement. A jamais !

V

Assis, accoudé à ma table. Des souvenirs affluent dans ma tête. Montréal. Saint-Laurent.[55] Merveille de la nature. Capricieux. Terre des hommes. Globe-Mappemonde coiffé de soleils. Confluent de toutes les races. Acharnement contre une. Faiblesse n'est pas force. Livrée à l'incommunicabilité des êtres séparés par les murs de l'argent, des mythes pseudo-justificatifs, scientifiques.

Mon esprit détruit les espaces. Enjambe les océans. Vogue dans les hauteurs. Me voilà à Paris, patrie brumeuse. Salle comble. Conférence. Icare vole haut. Me voilà à Moscou. A Tokyo. A New York. A Nice, Côted'Azur. Chance de la malchance. Brume. Le soleil rit derrière les nuages.

Où suis-je ? Dans mon bureau. Des bouquins épars. Quelques brouillons. Symbole de mon esprit brouillon. D'habitude prompt aux solutions les plus inattendues, aujourd'hui je me sens lâché par la nature entière en deuil. L'échec... Le mot maudit a failli rouler dans ma bouche. L'impuissance du génie est le deuil de la nature. La nuit à l'horizon, symbole de la mort. Une phrase jaillie des profondeurs de l'écho rôde dans ma tête sur un air de

55. A district on the outskirts of Montreal noted for its immigrant population.

plain-chant : « Quand est mort le poète, le monde entier… »[56] Mes yeux s'ébrouent. Il me semble que le monde entier fredonne cet air. Complices, toutes mes poules sont rentrées dans leur logis. Je ferme tous les rideaux. Me voilà entièrement emmuré. Entre quatre murs. Tapissés de livres. Sur la table, des portraits de toute la famille. Ma femme radieuse. Deux yeux-soleils brillants. Bouche lyrique. Poésie noire. Chef-d'œuvre de la nature. Œuvre de génie. Réussite d'art. Mes yeux sautillent et se trouvent face à face avec le portrait de Lautréamont juché mollement au-dessus de l'armoirebibliothèque.[57] Dieu de l'écriture. A l'instant muet. Complice lui aussi ? Non. Compatissant seulement. Entre génies seules les condoléances sont permises. L'écho me monte de nouveau telle une moutarde au nez. Au fond, il semble relayé par une voix de contre-alto qui rend tout dans la pièce lugubre. « Quand est mort le poète, le monde entier pleura. »

— Toc… toc… toc…

— Ouiii !

— Bonjour, Maître !

---

56. A quotation from the 1963 song "Quand il est mort, le poète," by the popular French singer Gilbert Bécaud, on the death of the writer and filmmaker Jean Cocteau.

57. Isidore Ducasse (1846–70), the self-styled Comte de Lautréamont, was a dissolute Uruguayan French poet beloved of the surrealists. He filled his poems with quotations from other writers and argued that all poetry is plagiarism.

— Ah, c'est toi ! Tu m'as fait peur, Niaiseux ! Quelle bonne nouvelle !

— Elles sont mauvaises, plutôt.

— Quoi ?

— Elle vient de tomber dans les télescripteurs du monde entier, relayée en chœur par toutes les agences de presse et toutes les radios : « dénonciation unilatérale de toutes les conventions africano-européo-humanitaires de coopération ». La radio nationale pompe à l'instant avec une violence inouïe ! Nouveau coup d'éclat. Nouvelle étape vers l'indépendance du pays !

— Chez les Coopérants ?

— Consternation générale ! Nuit noire !

— Il ne me reste plus qu'à démissionner.

— Moi aussi. Je te suis.

— Je ne voudrais pas vivre l'agonie de l'Institut. Partager devant l'histoire l'incapacité des africanolâtres à se gouverner ; leur inaptitude à la recherche scientifique.

— Il est temps de nous en aller. Sais-tu que l'autre camp siffle en ces heures douloureuses : « Tu as peur d'assumer des responsabilités. » Mlle Castino Paqua prépare tes cours ; te rédige le courrier bref, elle est ta respiration. Si elle part, c'est ton éclipse lente jusqu'à ta mort fatale. Davantage. Tes essais sont en fait une mystification de premier ordre. Étalage faussement savant d'une érudition trompeuse. Plagiat. Bavardage. Lieux communs.

Procédés à la base ? Des comptes rendus accumulés de la revue *Culture et développement* non cités.[58]

Tes poésies ? L'auteur ! Mademoiselle Castino Paqua. On y retrouve une phrase glanée par-ci par-là de tous les grands poètes. Des traductions du latin déguisées, présentées comme des phrases originales. Des poètes latins pillés. Catulle serait l'auteur le plus endommagé par tes escroqueries.

Davantage. Sartre, Althusser, héritiers légitimes de Marx et Lénine vont être saisis. Tes crimes doivent être dénoncés. Plusieurs éditeurs sont d'ores et déjà touchés pour une concertation commune sur la ligne de conduite à suivre. L'affaire prend donc des proportions tentaculaires. Chaque partie lésée revendique. L'Opinion publique s'émeut de tes viols. Sur la rue tu t'es permis de l'associer dans tes entreprises criminelles. Ton « Open Door » serait l'appareil savamment organisé pour ce qu'on qualifie de « la plus abominable escroquerie morale du siècle ». Des amateurs auraient ainsi écrit tout un roman de deux cents, trois cents pages. Tu y aurais apposé ta signature. La chose présentée sous des dehors démocratiques n'est en fait qu'une mystification de l'Opinion publique.

---

58. Echoing the name of the Belgian social science journal *Cultures et développement*.

Sur le plan politique. De telles initiatives sont inquiétantes. Assimilées à l'aliénation du peuple. On pense t'accuser de manœuvre habile d'asservissement de petites gens. Tu te livres à la subversion sur la voie publique. Qu'est-ce que cette guerre que tu mènes contre les idées reçues, toutes faites ? Tu veux ouvertement basculer la morale traditionnelle pour lui substituer ta morale à toi, coulée dans des appellations pompeuses d'« idées progressistes », « morale de la sincérité », « morale de la liberté ».

Davantage. L'accusation la plus grave serait l'incitation du peuple à des pratiques aliénantes. Ta liaison avec Mademoiselle Castino Paqua dont les théories érotiques — à vrai dire contre-nature — sont bien connues, serait à l'origine de cette accusation. Quelques citations tirées du catéchisme de ton amie sont spécialement mises en évidence :

> « L'érotisme est capable d'aider à la découverte d'un nouveau monde. »
> « Plus que cela : il est le progrès. »
> « L'homme érotique sera un nouvel animal. »
> « Les tabous de la morale bourgeoise sont d'origine économique. »
> « La société actuelle refoule et condamne à l'atrophie. »

« La loi nouvelle, la bonne loi, proclame qu'il est bel et bon de bien faire l'amour et de le faire librement. »

« La virginité n'est pas une vertu. »

« Le couple est une limite, le mariage une prison. »

« Il faut mettre le couple hors la loi. Il faut introduire un troisième personnage dans le couple. »

« Il faut constamment s'offrir, se donner, unir son corps à toujours plus de corps et tenir pour perdues les heures passées hors de leurs bras. »[59]

Voilà quelques échantillons. Il semble qu'ils ont épinglé plus de cinq cents propositions. L'accusation met l'accent sur l'aspect aliénant des pratiques auxquelles conduit cette doctrine insolite en Afrique.

Davantage. On aurait surpris ton amie en train de catéchiser des Africaines, exemples à l'appui. Elle-même s'exhibe ; se donne en spectacle. Quel spectacle ? Contre nature. Seule ou avec une autre. Toi, tu es associé à tous ces exercices acrobatiques. Tu pratiquerais cette sorte de catch.

Davantage. Ton mépris affiché pour les Nègres. Ton antiafricanisation de l'Institut. Ton incitation de certains

---

59. All of these quotations are taken from the novel *Emmanuelle*.

Nationaux et Coopérants à se rebeller contre les décisions des supérieurs.

Tous ces griefs se colportent de bouche à bouche et se répandent, alimentés comme par des vagues d'océans, ce qu'ils appellent la radio-trottoir. Commentés, amplifiés.

— Mon cher Niaiseux, le chien aboie, la caravane passe. Mon génie ne souffrira plus longtemps la négraille. Qu'y a-t-il de commun entre elle et moi ; et nous ? Nous sommes à l'instant, enfermés dans ce bureau. Nous nous comprenons. Tente la même expérience avec elle. C'est comme si tu franchissais un abîme. La foule, stupide par nature parce qu'irraisonnable, est incapable de s'associer au projet le plus révolutionnaire jamais conçu. Sous d'autres cieux, je serais aujourd'hui à la une des journaux. Me voilà réduit à néant.

— D'habitude, vous menez la partie. A présent nuit noire. Tu réussis toujours à jouer à la victime. A retourner les choses en ta faveur. L'Opinion publique, facilement maniable, mène le jeu. La balle est maintenant entre ses mains. Aujourd'hui, elle répond à l'attente que tu voulais d'elle. « L'Open Door », tu la cherches ; on te la sert. On dirait que tes ennemis sont dans la rue, dans les maisons, derrière les portes. Ils composent le scénario qu'en vain ton génie ne réussit pas à agencer. Tu veux donner à la foule, à la masse, une grande responsabilité.

L'ironie du sort veut qu'elle se la donne. Ton génie tente de créer un véritable sentiment de participation, de double courant. Le peuple te comprend. Tu démocratises les structures de communication, tu les révolutionnes ; tu en fais un véhicule de valeurs, allant de l'Opinion vers toi. Tu y as réussi. Tu n'as jamais autant réussi qu'en ces heures douloureuses. Tu as réussi sans le vouloir, à jeter ce pont sur le gouffre séparant la foule indéterminée et toi, écrivain. Tu veux sortir l'écrivain de sa solitude, la foule te mène sur la place publique. Ce roman auquel tu tiens à associer celleci, tu l'écriras. Avec des lettres d'or. Sous les cieux vers lesquels elle te conduira. Ici, la radio-trottoir a autant d'importance que le ministère public qui accuse. C'est elle qui veille sur la sécurité de l'État. Qui dépiste les ennemis. Qui décide du sort à leur réserver. Elle est toute puissante. Une force anonyme. Une machine infernale. Incontrôlable. Implacable. Avant qu'on ne s'aperçoive du bien-fondé d'une accusation, elle a déjà agi. Frappé haut. Son verdict est souvent irrémédiable.

Les amis ? Ne compte pas là-dessus. Dès qu'on sent la fumée, tous se retirent. Chacun soigne sa place. Y compris les Coopérants qui ont tout perdu dans ce pays. L'intérêt, c'est finalement le véritable médium entre les humains. Tu étais pour eux le tout-puissant ; la providence ; le père. Aujourd'hui tu es sale Nègre parmi les Nègres. Nègrement nègre. Oh, non ! Tu n'est pas un

Nègre. Tu es bien haut. Ton étoile n'a rien de noir. Elle brille même quand elle est éteinte.

— Les malheurs sont faits pour que les humains se comprennent. Non pour engendrer la pitié. Elle n'existe pas. Pour nous révéler à Nous-mêmes la relation d'existence à existence ; l'abîme qui sépare les êtres, leur opacité.

Le glas a sonné. Que reste-t-il du génie ? La force d'âme. Quand bien même il aura tout perdu. Léguer à la postérité le courage face au présent est un livre impérissable. L'histoire est pleine d'exemples. Les plus grands génies français ce ne sont peut-être pas ceux qu'on appelle écrivains dans le sens habituel du terme, mais ceux qui ont marqué la patrie des Jeanne d'Arc, des Napoléon, par leur grandeur d'âme. Le courage immortalise.

Deuxième Partie

VI

Nous voilà hors du temps des humains. Nous y sommes, nous y resterons. La pièce a à peine deux mètres sur trois et quatre de haut. Juste de quoi ne pas étouffer. Les murs lisses. Pas une seule fenêtre. Huis-clos parfait.

— Si je comprends bien, nous sommes déjà dans l'éternité sans y être ?

— L'immobilité du temps !

— Oui, sans montre ! Les jours et les nuits, tous pareils.

— C'est votre rêve réalisé !

— Pas dans les circonstances que j'aurais souhaitées.

— Je m'inquiète du sort qu'on vous réserve, Maître ! Le cachot peut durer quatre, cinq mois comme il peut demander plusieurs années. Mais je compte quelques mois.

— Pourvu qu'un jugement intervienne.

— J'imagine qu'un interrogatoire précédera le jugement. Ce n'est pas toujours le cas, paraît-il ! Des fois, on relâche sans jugement. On estime dans ce cas que vous vous êtes corrigé de ce dont on vous accuse.

— Mais dans notre cas qui accuse ? L'Opinion publique ? De quoi nous accuse-t-on ?

— Nous pouvons le savoir par l'intermédiaire du geôlier.

— Si nous avons la chance d'en rencontrer un. Il n'est pas non plus sûr qu'il connaisse les griefs à notre charge.

— Quelle que soit l'issue, Maître, mon plus grand bonheur est d'avoir été associé de si près à votre sort. Il n'est pas donné à tout le monde de vivre les derniers moments d'un génie. C'est le plus beau livre que l'on puisse lire !

— Ma vie, Niaiseux, par elle-même est en somme un livre ! La postérité me rendra — et me rend déjà — ce témoignage auquel j'ai droit.

— Les grands hommes ont toujours, au soir de leur vie, confié leurs derniers souvenirs. Pensez à Socrate. Sans la présence de Platon, nous n'aurions jamais rien connu de sa doctrine ni de son enseignement. Le sort nous place aujourd'hui côte à côte. Des jours, des mois durant, nous aurons à respirer le même air ; à vivre les mêmes inquiétudes ; les mêmes angoisses. Si par impossible je vous survis, je suis le seul témoin qui pourrait relater vos derniers instants. Votre pensée lumineuse au moment suprême serait recueillie par celui qui toute sa vie vous aura voué un culte jusqu'au-delà de la tombe. Je vous prie de me livrer votre dernière pensée.

— Cher ami, une chose est certaine : je ne renie rien de mes credo. Je ne suis pas un Lévy-Bruhl qui, au soir de sa vie, revient sur ses propres dogmes.[60] Je ne me chauffe pas de ce bois-là. Nous nous trouvons par la force des choses enfermés ici comme dans une matrice. Espace primordial. Mon rêve. Réceptacle. Caverne. Vase. Outre. Nous y sommes à l'instant installés non par un désir quelconque jailli de notre vouloir-vivre mais par une agressivité mâle. Je ne le regrette pas. Celleci, nous place dans une métaphore qui répond bien à ce qu'aura été le rêve de ma vie. Suave ironie qui lie le génie et le délivre des contingences. On entre, dans ce creux, avec des lettres dorées par le courage.

Jamais tu n'as été aussi doctoral qu'aujourd'hui. Tes paroles coulent à pic en moi. Nous atrophier ! Nous rendre impuissants ! Mais la virilité intellectuelle est plus que trop forte. La lucidité plus qu'aiguisée. On nous réduit à l'état de rechercher d'être aimés plus que d'aimer. On nous rejette. C'est ça le symbole de ce creux, de cette cavité, de ce néant. Néant cependant de plénitude. Je me possède. Je ne suis plus des leurs. Leur temps nous est soustrait. Ils nous

---

60. In a posthumously published notebook, *Les carnets* (1949), the French ethnographer Lucien Lévy-Bruhl contemplated abandoning the theory of pre-logical thought that he had advanced in works such as *La mentalité primitive* (1922).

refusent le passé et l'avenir. Ils nous condamnent au présent. Tu ne peux plus dire hier, aujourd'hui, demain. Les Esquimaux au pôle Nord ont encore droit à l'été indien. Nous, tout cela, nous est refusé. Présent ! Éternel présent, je t'adore ! Je t'invoque. Je t'aime. Tu es là. Ta présence jamais interrompue est la seule compagne qui me soit donnée. Fidèle. Tu me combles.

— Maître, vous avez beaucoup voyagé, rencontré des humains. Quelle est votre pensée la plus profonde sur eux ?

— L'humain me paraît toujours comme ce qu'on hume. Partout où tu passes, tu humes, tu humes ! Mais tu ne parviens pas à le respirer. L'odeur, tu la sens, mais la substance te reste invisible, insaisissable. L'homme est pour son semblable un parfum. Précieux, s'il parvient à établir entre lui et celui-ci une détente. Nocif, si c'est l'état de tension qui s'installe. Il recherche toujours la détente. C'est pourquoi il n'est jamais au repos. Il ne se livre aux autres que par la loi de l'intérêt qui revêt des formes multiples. L'amour, l'argent, l'asservissement. L'indifférence est elle-même aussi l'expression d'un intérêt masqué. Malraux a, dans une fulgurance, dit : « Qu'est-ce que l'homme ? Un tas de petits secrets. »[61] Moi, je te dis, « un tas de petits intérêts ».

---

61. In his novel *Les noyers de l'Altenburg* (1945), André Malraux wrote, "Pour l'essentiel, l'homme est ce qu'il cache. . . . Un misérable petit tas de secrets" (54).

— Deux définitions, deux génies !

— Si tu veux ! Tu aimes des rapprochements ! C'est exact !

« Un tas de petits intérêts » enveloppé dans une épaisse opacité. C'est cela qui alourdit la condition humaine. Tu la lis sur tous les visages. Sur les lèvres de la vendeuse qui te sourit pour t'attirer vers ses marchandises ; dans les yeux de la personne aimée avec laquelle tu voudrais fusionner mais qui te reste éloignée par l'espace qui te sépare d'elle. C'est pourquoi ma vie est un combat perpétuel contre l'espace. Échapper à l'espace. Détruire l'espace. Vocation de toute vraie philosophie. Mon système ne vise qu'à cela. Relier ces « tas d'intérêts » par un lien qui transcende l'espace. L'écriture, ma vraie religion, je la veux ce lieu de transcendance. Toutes mes recherches tendent à fonder cette science nouvelle de l'écriture. L'écriture gestuelle, matrice de liberté et d'initiative tant pour l'écrivain que pour le lecteur. Plénitude de sens. Flux et reflux de la pensée souterraine. L'écrivain enfin sorti de la solitude. Le lecteur restitué à sa vraie personnalité : délivré de la passivité. L'écriture enfin laïcisée, c'est-à-dire, rendue démocratique. Laos, peuple. Le public devenu co-auteur avec l'écrivain, l'abîme qui sépare les deux enfin franchi. Abîme-espace ! Affreux ! Le monde réconcilié, et les antagonismes estompés. Quelle révolution ! Comme le poète maudit, je suis incompris.

Méconnu. Renié. Rejeté. Banni comme un brigand. Je ne veux que servir ce peuple, l'humanité. Me voilà traîné dans la boue. Pire qu'un criminel. L'Union des écrivains, une fois au courant de ce crime, protestera. Les philistins, à leur confusion, me relâcheront. Mais voilà que je me jette dans le futur. Fol espoir meurtrier ! Présent, où es-tu ? Reviens, reviens ! Non, tu es toujours là, Ami !

On introduit une clé dans la serrure. La porte s'ouvre. Une traînée de lumière envahit toute la pièce. Viol de notre solitude !

— Chiens d'étrangers, il paraît que vous voulez renverser le régime, en prêchant sur la voie publique la révolution !

Mes yeux ne semblent plus habitués à la lumière ; les oreilles supportent mal l'éclat de cette voix tonitruante du gardien. La porte se referme.

Un coup file tout droit sur la nuque de Niaiseux. Toi, fiente d'étrangers, comment oses-tu soutenir et exciter cet égaré qui se prend trop au sérieux ?

Niaiseux tombe tête première. Son menton heurte violemment le sol. Il gémit. En se relevant, deux de ses dents gisent blanches comme deux cristaux pourfendant le noir de la pièce. L'homme lui ordonne de les ramasser.

— Avale-les, chien ! enjoint-il.

Niaiseux les ramasse. S'exécute. L'homme s'acharne.

On ne brave pas impunément l'ordre établi par les ancêtres. Que l'homme blanc le viole, c'est compréhensible ! C'est dans sa nature de défier la nature. Qu'un fils du pays se porte complice, la colère des ancêtres le consumera.

Me regardant fixement, il crache par terre. Signe de suprême mépris. Un frisson d'indignation me parcourt la tête. L'écho d'une certaine voix me traverse vaguement. Les yeux de l'homme ne me quittent pas. Il semble être l'envoyé de quelqu'un ! Qui ? Et pourquoi ? Il se fait menaçant. Toute la pièce se remplit de bruits. Un coup d'une violence inouïe asséné à ma tête me renvoie contre un mur. Tout le cachot semble traversé par des points lumineux. Des étoiles filantes partent du centre pour aller bombarder la périphérie. Un deuxième coup me cloue au tapis. Je me relève. Je ne pousse pas un seul cri. Le vers du poète me revient à l'esprit : « Pleurer, gémir, prier, est également lâche. »[62] Je me retiens. Le monstre est toujours dans la pièce. Dans un coin. Fulminant. Ses deux proies ont, pour seule force à opposer, leur faiblesse. Combat inégal. Agneaux livrés sans défense.

---

62. From Alfred de Vigny's 1843 philosophical poem "La mort du loup" (*Œuvres* 100–02), which envisions a dying wolf telling his hunter to accept fate without complaining: "Gémir, pleurer, prier est également lâche" (102).

« Ne croyez pas, sales chiens, que nous tomberons dans le piège qui consacre des traîtres martyrs. Martyrs de quoi ? Toi de ta niaiserie. L'autre de son orgueil. Exploiter les siens pour servir l'étranger ! Oser s'adresser aux ancêtres en ne reculant devant aucune célébration traditionnelle pour égaler le Blanc. Taxer nos cérémonies de rites sauvages et les exploiter à des fins mercantiles ! Piétiner toute la sagesse ancestrale ! La traiter de fétichisme ! Crimes irrémissibles ! Tu entends ! L'enfant qui renie sa mère n'a droit à aucun regard de pitié. Nous avons été bravés, de nuit, de jour. Toutes tes conversations avec tes soi-disant Coopérants nous les avons suivies jour pour jour.

Le mépris que tu étales sur nous, sur le genre humain, sale monstre, nous le subissons. Les séances d'initiation, les as-tu oubliées, grand écrivain ? Les avertissements, les prémonitions, tu n'en as pas tenu compte. Cérémonies sauvages, sans doute ! Tu as dérangé nos sommeils ; celui de nos morts. Insulté nos dieux ! sacrilège !

L'espace que tu recherches ! c'est pour y vivre avec les Blancs seulement ? Les Nègres n'y ayant aucune place ! Tu les as exclus du genre humain. Quel mal t'ontils fait. Ils sont paisibles. Ils t'ont tout donné y compris la possibilité de les rejeter. Ne devrais-tu pas aller dans une clinique de transfusion sanguine, dans une « banque de sang », vider ton sang entièrement et le troquer contre du sang blanc ! Pousse la logique jusqu'au bout. Un voyage jusqu'au bout de la nuit à la Céline ?[63] Une piqûre. Et, en un clin d'œil, tu es blanc ! Quant aux autres attributs de la négritude, une opération esthétique viendrait à bout des imperfections restantes : l'épatement du nez ; l'épaisseur des lèvres ; la couleur des yeux ; la crépitude des cheveux ! Tu ne vois la possibilité de développement de l'être humain que dans la "blanchitude". Hors de là, point de salut. Régression. Animalité. Contre-nature. Contre-culture. Archaïsme. Préhistoire. Mentalité primitive. Royaume des mythes. Fatalités. Contraintes.

Pousse ta logique. Tu es dans l'histoire. Nous, nous sommes hors de l'histoire. Peut-être au-dessus de l'histoire. Tu recours à nous pour "décoller". T'es-tu interrogé sur la possibilité même de communication entre des étapes de l'humanité aussi "différentes" ? Aussi "distantes" de plusieurs millions d'années-lumière ? L'abîme est infranchissable entre ton discours et le nôtre. Pourquoi, Savant, as-tu tenté la démarche ? Notre discours se nourrit des mythes, des légendes. Notre logique s'appuie sur des proverbes. Quelle plateforme de dialogue

---

63. In Louis-Ferdinand Céline's novel *Voyage au bout de la nuit* (1932), the antihero Bardamu wanders through the battlefields of World War I, the jungles of colonial Africa, and industrial Detroit before finally settling in Paris as a doctor to the poor.

peux-tu fournir entre toi et nous ? Ton discours est un tissu de références à des philosophies étrangères, à des modes de pensée labourés par tous les débordements, les pires subversions et le relâchement des mœurs. Ton aliénation ne réside pas dans le fait de nous avoir quittés. Mais dans la tentative de reboisement de ton identité. L'Europe déplumée essaie de repiquer des espaces entiers pour donner l'illusion de forêts. Son histoire est devenue nostalgie permanente de ce qu'elle a perdu. Y a-t-il jamais eu de paradis perdus ? Du moins l'Occident entretient-il cette illusion par une abondante littérature. Toi, tu nous quittes. Tu coupes tout lien psychologique avec nous. Tu crées artificiellement un refoulement du naturel en toi. Pour te libérer, tu oses t'adresser encore à nous ! Perçois-tu la contradiction ? As-tu oublié tous les saints européens qui pourraient te venir en aide ? Jean-Jacques Rousseau. Bernardin de Saint Pierre.[64] Chateaubriand dont ta tête est fortement entichée ? Non seulement professeurs mais aussi héros de l'ensauvagement ! Génie, identifie-toi héroïquement à eux ! Tu redeviendras bruissant d'arbres ! »

---

64. Bernardin de Saint Pierre is best known for his novel *Paul et Virginie* (1788), set on the island of Mauritius in the Indian Ocean. In terms echoing Jean-Jacques Rousseau's *Discours sur l'origine et les fondements de l'inégalité parmi les hommes* (1755), the novel contrasts life in a pure state of nature with the corruption of French society.

L'homme rouvre la porte. La referme brutalement. Pendant tout son discours, mes jambes sont comme paralysées. La douleur du coup rude reçu de sa droite est suspendue. Je la ressens de nouveau. Niaiseux se couche. S'endort-il réellement ? Je n'ose le réveiller. Pourquoi le déranger ? Ma tête me fait tellement mal que toute concentration est impossible. L'angoisse me saisit. Une vengeance se prépare sans doute ! Laquelle ? Sous quelles formes ? Des tortures physiques ? Des humiliations ? Ou les deux ? Combien de temps demeurerons-nous ici ? Simples épreuves ? Initiation ? La pédagogie de la souffrance commence. Je sens le vide le plus absolu en moi. Tout voyage intérieur, absurde ! Sans terme. Sans profondeur. La vie m'apparaît pour la première fois comme l'envers de cette plénitude qui me définit toujours. La violence nous guette. La violence nous cerne de toutes parts. Mâle. Menaçante. Instinctuelle. Mythique… Rituelle. Nourricière. Les peuples s'en nourrissent. Nous voilà victimes expiatoires. Amène métaphore ! Oui, métaphore ! La culture se meurt en moi pour qu'elle renaisse. Je me fais le point zéro pour qu'elle se fasse fondatrice. Oh violence sacrée me voici prêt,[65] tel un Socrate ! Toi, au moins

---

65. Viko here echoes the ideas of the critic and anthropologist René Girard. In *La violence et le sacré* (1972) Girard proposed that culture is based on primal acts of ritual violence and that Christianity uniquely advocates self-sacrifice rather than the sacrifice of others.

tu es la seule à me comprendre. Je désire ce rendez-vous inscrit dans la fatalité. Je t'adore. Je me prostitue pour toi. Toute culture vient de toi. Le langage ; l'imaginaire ; les sociétés. Tu es mère de tout. Tu gouvernes tout. Tu es la vraie reine. La vraie refoulée. Tu m'immoleras. Me voici victime émissaire. Le vrai savoir. La vrai initiation. Point d'autre explication sacrificielle. Tu te suffis. L'homme est né de toi. La vérité humaine est ta fille. Ordre primordial où tout se rejoint. D'où tout prend racine.

— Maître, je ne dors pas. La douleur est tellement intense que j'ai l'impression que ma mâchoire inférieure va s'arracher. Je vous entends. Vos paroles sont lénifiantes. Jamais votre pensée n'a atteint une telle profondeur. On me présente toujours la violence comme un parasite. Et voilà que pour la première fois, elle m'apparaît sous une lumière lacanienne.[66] Il a fallu que vous soyiez au soir de votre vie pour que l'humanité bénéficie de cette grâce exceptionnelle.

— Non pas au soir de ma vie mais au printemps ! Je considère ces instants suprêmes comme la renaissance de ma vie ; de la culture. Le vrai saut de la nature. La culture n'est rien d'autre que cela. La nature bondissant hors d'elle-même ; se dédoublant. Elle est comme le rap-

66. The psychoanalyst Jacques Lacan (1901–81) argued for the transformative power of a violent rupture of one's thoughts and identity.

port du réel à l'imaginaire.[67] Ce saut primaire, c'est la violence qui l'accomplit. La culture est portée par une violence constante. Elle s'engendre dans la violence. Elle nourrit toutes les mutations socio-économiques, politiques, de violence.

— Une telle théorie ne cache-t-elle pas de l'ambiguïté.

— Comme toutes les intuitions profondes ! Il n'y a pas appel ici à la violence ni au totalitarisme. Mais une sacralisation de la matrice comme possibilité même de la nature humaine à s'accomplir dans le dépassement d'elle-même. Nature, bien sûr, au sens historique du terme. Il n'y a pas lieu de penser ici au concept desséchant des scolastiques thomistes.[68] Toi qui as l'insigne chance de vivre ces instants uniques, si la tourmente ne t'emporte pas avec moi, je te considère comme le légataire universel de ma pensée. Qu'on ne la gauchisse pas !

— Quelle lourde responsabilité ! Il faudrait votre génie pour pouvoir la maintenir à l'abri des malversations intellectuelles de vos ennemis.

Ce n'est pas cela l'important. L'essentiel, c'est que l'humanité recueille l'étincelle de vérité qui lui est offerte.

---

67. In Lacan's theory, developed in his *Écrits* and elsewhere, *the real* is the natural state from which we are cut off by language; *the imaginary* is a fantasy that is meant to compensate for the self's fundamental state of lack and the self's loss of the real.

68. Medieval Neoplatonist academics, followers of Thomas Aquinas.

Le canal, c'est toi. Si tu es emporté en même temps que moi, les misérables humains manquent une chance qui ne s'offrira peut-être plus jamais.

— Chut ! Quelqu'un arrive !

La porte s'ouvre. Un homme à la carrure d'un orang-outang pénètre. Niaiseux se redresse. Je lui fais signe de garder son sang-froid. Notre dernier moment, fis-je ! Un seul coup suffira à régler notre compte. Visage de masque. Aurait-il quelque relation avec une vision eue la veille dans mon bureau ? Deux dents très pointues ornent les deux extrémités de sa bouche. Est-ce un tueur envoyé pour inspecter les lieux ? Quelle sorte de mort nous réserve-t-on ? Étranglement ? Pendaison ? Simple coup de pistolet ? L'homme n'a rien sur lui. Il n'a pas besoin d'arme. Saurait-il le manier, si on lui en offrait ? Il semble situé à la limite entre l'animal et l'homme.

Il nous regarde tour à tour fixement. Regard interrogateur et un peu stupidement étonné. Comme pour dire : ça ne vaut pas la peine. Deux mouches ! Ses yeux parcourent toute la pièce. Que cherche-t-il ? Nous sommes pétrifiés d'effroi. Qu'il en finisse, me dis-je intérieurement. Il respire un moment profondément. Une odeur âcre emplit la pièce. S'il reste longtemps, pensé-je, il va nous vider le peu d'oxygène. Puis un regard de profond mépris. Et il referme la porte. Sans mot dire, il s'en va.

— Allons-nous revivre ici le théâtre de mon bureau ? Avec cette différence que je ne suis plus meneur de jeu ? Suis-je vraiment prisonnier ou ce chef d'orchestre de toujours ? Eux, ils ont l'illusion de disposer de moi. Mais c'est moi en fait qui dispose d'eux ! Ils vont défiler pour la danse macabre.[69] Je les fais danser. Leurs émotions, leurs ressentiments, leurs instincts déchaînés sont des animateurs de cette partouze avec laquelle nous avons rendez-vous. L'inspirateur, c'est moi. Sans moi tout cela n'aurait pas lieu. J'aurais été pour l'humanité jusqu'au dernier moment sa chance.

— C'est énigmatique, l'attitude de cette espèce d'homo sapiens ! J'ai cru que d'un moment à l'autre nous ne serions plus qu'un paquet de souvenirs pour l'humanité !

— Dans un tel individu : il n'y a pas deux langages. Un seul, la force physique. La nature l'a bien doté d'une richesse brute. C'est de la matière première, qui a besoin d'être transformée. Il vit ce stade primaire caractérisé par l'absence du dédoublement culturel. Spéculum de l'autre homme.[70]

---

69. *La danse macabre* was a medieval allegory in which skeletons escorted humans to their graves; that allegory is the subject of *Danse macabre* (1874), a famous tone poem by Camille Saint-Saëns.

70. A play on *Speculum de l'autre femme* (1974), by the Lacanian feminist Luce Irigaray, who criticized the phallocentrism of Western philosophy and psychology from Aristotle to Freud.

— Comment y accédera-t-il ?

— Chez de tels individus, le pouvoir auto-créateur est si faible ou si affaibli par l'environnement social qu'il leur doit être insufflé de l'extérieur. Je ne nie pas en lui l'humanité mais elle est noyée ; écrasée par la pesanteur des fatalités animales.

— Mais a-t-il la possibilité de s'ouvrir à ce souffle extérieur ?

— Il s'agirait de le sortir de l'intimité avec la nature ; de le rendre en somme traître du secret qui le lie sans façon à la terre, aux étoiles, aux plantes, aux bêtes ; de le faire célébrer le quotidien pétri de rationalité. Non de rationalité desséchante telle qu'elle est vécue en Occident. Mais de rationalité où la raison et la nature ont chacune sa part. Suprême sagesse !

— En somme une infusion de rationalité dans la nature !

— Oui ! Il s'agit d'un dosage. Ni hypermysticisme ni hyperrationalité. L'un et l'autre dénaturent l'homme.

— Qui serait capable d'une telle opération ?

— Il s'agit moins d'un corps de connaissances données de l'extérieur que d'une insertion du prétendu « présent ethnographique » — le mot je ne l'aime pas beaucoup[71]

---

71. Viko shares this dislike with the anthropologist Johannes Fabian, who taught at the University of Zaire in 1973; in *Time and the Other* (1983), Fabian criticizes ethnographers who present primitive cultures

— de l'Afrique dans le présent de notre mouvement de l'histoire ; dans la dialectique des déterminismes mythiques et de la liberté. L'insertion dans cette dialectique est chose faite ; mais il faudrait en accélérer le mouvement. Ce qui le freine, c'est une soi-disant révolution culturelle qui fait émerger et entretient pêle-mêle, vieilles habitudes, vieilles coutumes, vieilles idées justifiables certes dans l'univers mythique mais inconsistantes dans le monde moderne. Le passé n'est pas à nier. Il est une entité intérieure à nous. Il ne doit être pris en considération que dans son rapport au présent. Mais ceci ne relève pas d'une décision uniquement politique. Bien des coutumes africaines ne résistent pas au choc du présent et du futur. Une sélection spontanée en aura raison. C'est alors qu'une certaine forme de rationalité s'installera bon gré mal gré. Dialectique du succès et de l'insuccès ou de l'échec de la maintenance à tout prix de telle ou telle coutume dégradante. Il se réalisera ce qu'on pourrait appeler « une coupure épistémologique » qui fera voir aux Africains le réel avec un regard neuf ; leur fera traiter le temps et l'espace — maîtres mots — de manière prospective. Travail souterrain, patient, de la taupe.

---

by writing in an "ethnographic present" outside the flow of history (80).

VII

Trêve de paroles. Niaiseux souffre terriblement en silence. Philosophiquement. Moi-même, quand je cesse de parler, j'ai l'impression que mon cerveau va éclater. Pas de soupir. Pas un seul gémissement.

La serrure grince de nouveau. La porte s'ouvre. Entre un homme vêtu de peau de chèvre ; les biceps entourés de bracelets en argent. La tête couverte d'un chapeau entièrement en perles, couronné de plumes de perroquet. Il est suivi d'un beau jeune homme élégamment habillé. La porte se referme derrière eux. Cependant, la pièce qui, une fois la porte fermée, est sombre, reste cette fois-ci éclairée. Le foyer de lumière est invisible.

En un éclair je comprends la raison de notre huis-clos. Mes audaces au bureau produisent maintenant leurs effets. Mais je me garde d'en souffler mot à Niaiseux.

L'homme se tourne vers le jeune homme. Lui parle longuement. A son tour le jeune homme nous traduit :

« Chiens de chiens, fils de chiens ! Ma dignité, mon honneur m'interdisent de m'adresser directement à vous. Votre crime est incommensurable. Vous l'expierez jusqu'à la dernière goutte de votre sang. Mais n'aspirez cependant pas à être considérés comme des martyrs. Vous n'aurez pas cet honneur.

« La raison fondamentale qui m'interdit de vous interpeller directement est que nos univers ne se rencontrent pas ; la parole et l'écriture. Vous avez irrévérencieusement mis entre vous et nous un abîme. Vous avez choisi l'univers du livre — l'espace scriptural — abandonnant celui qui a nourri votre enfance ; alimenté vos rêves ; meublé votre subconscient. Vous avez prétendu expulser ce lac profond de symboles, d'images, noyau où se soude la cohésion culturelle de notre communauté. Nous sommes pour vous de parfaits étrangers. Nous avons suivi votre aliénation avec un cœur gros. Mais nous savions que vous n'iriez pas très loin, qu'une nostalgie vous ramènerait sur nos rivages. Les richesses sacrées de l'oralité rejetées dédaigneusement laissent toujours sur les coupables une odeur qui les poursuit comme un remords rongeur. La gravité de votre impiété réside dans la tentative de désacralisation de l'oralité. La liberté, l'espace, le temps du conteur, vous avez voulu les réapprivoiser ; les introduire dans le discours romanesque. Démarche athée, dépourvue de foi. N'étant pas parvenu au résultat criminel escompté, vous avez poussé la présomption jusqu'à vous laisser initier à nos rites, espérant ainsi arriver au but. Ce faisant, vous introduisiez de la subversion dans l'oralité et dans le discours occidental. Vous alliez accoucher des personnages, des héros, des textes hybrides. C'est pourquoi ce sacrilège ne peut rester impuni.

« Mais auparavant on vous administrera la potion de vérité qui vous fera avouer tous vos autres crimes contre l'humanité. Tout ce que vous avez organisé à l'Institut comme méfaits, il vous faut les désavouer. Les Noirs de l'Institut sont des êtres humains au même titre que les Coopérants. Vous ne les considérez pas comme des humains. Ce n'est pas la peau qui fait la valeur d'un homme ni son érudition mais ce qui jusqu'à présent vous a échappé. J'ai dit. »

Ce discours si persuasif me vainc par la force de son évidence. Pour la première fois l'opposition oraiité/écriture m'apparaît dans une lumière violemment inattendue. Si celle-là impose la loi du sacré, celle-ci le fait du profane. Le langage écrit n'est donc pas une variante du langage oral. Deux univers ayant chacun une histoire qui se perd au fond des âges. Trajectoires opposées. Deux types d'humanité, cependant... non inconciliables !

Le jeune homme témoigne d'une haute culture. Son discours d'une clarté aveuglante et didactique est-il une traduction ou un commentaire brodé tendancieusement par lui ? Me dis-je !

Notre sort est donc réglé. Quelques minutes de silence... Il va falloir payer mon impiété. En un éclair,

Michelet voyait la France et son âme debout ;[72] moi, Giambatista, je vois la mienne s'effondrer ; *my way of life* se dissoudre comme du soufre dans l'eau. Afrique, tu es vainqueur ! Non, tu ne l'es pas encore ! Tu n'as pas le dernier mot. Le premier, tu l'as cependant : le chemin, en effet, vers la renaissance à la vie commence par le réchauffement de la foi en soi-même.

L'homme fait signe au jeune homme pour l'inviter à sortir de la pièce. Après un instant, celui-ci revient avec une cruche. Un nouveau signe. Le jeune homme s'approche de moi. Et d'un geste sec m'invite à boire méthodiquement. A vider la cruche en trois prises. A moi de faire la répartition. Pourquoi trois fois ? Une lecture faite au hasard me revient à la tête. La connaissance profonde de l'Afrique passe par l'interprétation des signes et des symboles. C'est à la simple surface des choses qu'on nage si, écrivain africain, on se contente seulement de célébrer le continent dans ses angoisses, ses peines, ses ressentiments, ses frustrations, ses refoulements, ses désirs profonds et ardents, ses joies. L'écriture doit se

---

72. In the preface to his *Histoire de France* (1869), Jules Michelet wrote that his massive project was conceived in a flash of insight when he perceived France "comme une âme et une personne" (1: 45). Appropriately, Michelet was strongly influenced by Vico, whose *Scienza nuova* he translated into French.

faire elle-même signe et symbole, univers de correspondances. Fulgurance d'un moment de ravissement que mon génie vit avant de mourir. La parole de Gœthe me revient : « Arrête-toi, instant, tu es si beau. »[73] Passé vainqueur, caresse-moi. Présent, ravis-moi. Espace, dilate-moi. Que je meure en vous. Que je renaisse en vous !

Où me mène-t-on, tel un mouton vers l'abattoir ? Serait-ce vers la vraie initiation, tel un intrépide navigateur le long des fleuves, au large des mers et des océans ?

Je me conforme aux injonctions. Des coups de bâtons rythment les trois prises. L'effet semble se produire lentement. Progressivement. Petit à petit mes yeux deviennent sans doute hagards pour ceux qui me regardent. Les formes perdent leur netteté. Le bourdonnement des oreilles commence. Un concert de discours grinçants et discordants s'installe en moi.

Halluciné du réel et de l'imaginaire ? Oui, sagesse. Je vois des monstres. Des crapauds. Des sauterelles dévorer des fourmis. Trois coups secs sur mes épaules et à la colonne vertébrale me jettent à genoux. Et je commence à vomir des grenouilles très visqueuses. Des crabes. A la

---

73. In Johann Wolfgang von Goethe's *Faust* (1808), when Faust makes his pact with the devil, he agrees that if Mephistopheles gives him anything that pleases him so much that he wants to stay in the moment forever, he will die at that instant (49).

fin plus qu'un liquide visqueux. Je ne perds cependant pas ma lucidité.

— Étranger, tu vas maintenant confesser tes crimes contre l'humanité. La potion de vérité t'a rendu la tâche facile. Tu es dans l'impossibilité de nous cacher quoi que ce soit. Ta lucidité est à sens unique. C'est-à-dire que sur une vérité proférée, il n'est plus possible d'y revenir. C'est l'immédiateté pure ! Machine à détecter la vérité. Sale chien d'étranger, tu constates bien que nous n'avons pas besoin d'appareillage compliqué enchaînant la tête de l'individu dans une foule d'encéphalogrammes. Comme il n'y a plus pour nous danger que le secret soit trahi, je peux te l'expliquer simplement. Les bestioles que tu as vu sortir de ton estomac ont été administrées dans la potion de vérité. Les crabes ont eu pour mission de gratter les parois de l'estomac, de blesser certaines fibres en liaison avec les fibres nerveuses. La douleur qui s'ensuivit aurait été normalement atroce si nous n'avions administré en même temps des grenouilles dont la mission était de sécréter un liquide lénifiant qui répare toutes blessures presque instantanément. Voilà toute la vérité dans sa simplicité étonnamment simple.

Par ailleurs, le genre de fautes que tu confesseras nous permettra de voir si ta conscience est normale.

Vas-y maintenant.

— J'avoue m'être associé activement aux manœuvres basses de mes deux sinistres collègues Haïna et Malawi, pour « couler » un étudiant innocent. Par ailleurs, je méprise profondément ces deux collègues. Le premier pour son incompétence qui tient la une des conversations des étudiants. Plus souvent aux chantiers de construction que dans les auditoires des cours, cet individu a un diplôme douteux, inclassable.

Certains de ses étudiants sont plus compétents que lui. Ses méthodes d'approche sont vieilles de quarante ans. Si méthodes il y a !

Quant à Malawi, il a un diplôme en ordre. Comme le premier, il est foncièrement tribaliste.

Depuis dix ans, les étudiants subissent des inepties qu'il brode autour de sa langue maternelle.

Je reconnais ma faute.

Je m'accuse de haïr un confrère de renommée internationale. Je ne peux digérer sa présence. Je suis fait pour être premier partout. J'ai pris ombrage de ses mérites. J'ai organisé avec l'aide des plus jeunes des actions diffamatoires contre lui. Les Coopérants ont été très habilement informés. Le résultat a été atteint. Moins de sympathie. Vide autour de lui. Davantage. J'ai fait régner la terreur. J'ai imposé une dictature intellectuelle au sein de l'Institut.

Je reconnais ma faute ma très grande faute.

Les Coopérants n'ont pas été épargnés. Pour moi c'étaient des purs instruments que j'ai utilisés soit pour combattre les Nationaux qui levaient la tête un peu trop haut soit pour exécuter des travaux à des fins personnelles. Les Coopérants sont aussi des humains. On ne peut les utiliser comme des instruments. L'humanité n'a pas de couleur.

Je reconnais ma très très grande faute.

Il est un cas parmi les Coopérants que je me dois de signaler spécialement. Voulant le foutre dehors, j'ai inventé sur lui les ignominies les plus invraisemblables.

Je reconnais ma trop trop grande faute.

Je n'ai épargné personne. Les Autorités ont eu leur part. J'ai excité des collègues contre elles. Ils y sont allés tête basse. Ma conduite est fondée sur l'hypocrisie et la perfidie. Pour moi mes chefs sont de parfaits imbéciles, hissés à leurs postes par des intérêts sordides.

Je reconnais ma trop grande faute.

Je hais le genre humain. J'ignore ce qu'est l'amitié. Une détente dans les rapports entre deux hommes ! Un ami, c'est celui qui reflète mon image. En somme, mon double.

Contre le genre humain, elle est irrémissible, ma faute.

Je la reconnais sans qualificatif.

— Parfait monstre ! Maintenant on va t'offrir un petit plaisir érotico-masochiste auquel ont droit tous ceux qui passent par la potion de vérité.

On fait entrer l'Orang-Outang. On lui désigne Niaiseux qui jusque-là n'a eu droit qu'au plaisir de spectateur. La partie active commence. L'homme fonce droit sur lui. Il connaît le métier pour l'avoir fait des centaines de fois. Il le saisit par les cheveux ; le soulève jusqu'à la hauteur de son visage et lui crache de plein fouet à la figure. Il le laisse retomber. Il le ressaisit ; le lance au plafond sans le rattraper. Niaiseux retombe lourdement comme un corps sans squelette. Pour la première fois de ma vie, j'ai un sentiment de pitié. Le spectacle m'arrache spontanément le cri : « C'est ça l'homme ! »[74] Mon cri attire à peine l'attention de l'assistance conquise par la cruauté de la scène.

On apporte à l'homme une grosse aiguille chauffée à blanc. Il déshabille brutalement Niaiseux. Il enfonce celle-ci à travers la queue de mon pauvre ami qui pousse un de ces cris, le plus horrible jamais proféré. Pour éviter une hémorragie, le bourreau met dans le trou laissé par l'aiguille une poudre noire. Il pousse l'ingéniosité encore plus loin jusqu'à y placer un anneau au bout duquel il suspend une petite clochette au son très aigu, pouvant s'entendre de très loin. Par ailleurs, la clochette permet à Niaiseux de ne rencontrer dans le couvent aucune

---

74. Viko's exclamation now replaces Buffon's aphorism "Le style, c'est l'homme."

personne du sexe opposé. Le tintement régulier de la clochette invite les femmes à se cacher au passage de Niaiseux. Symbole d'ignominie infligée aux traîtres.

Tous ces événements ont des répercussions dans les autres couvents. L'on décide de me confondre une fois pour toutes en me confrontant aux maîtres de la parole avant de me livrer au sort qui m'est réservé. Au procès, chacun des hauts lieux de la culture, de l'initiation et de l'occultisme sera représenté par son chef et un conseiller culturel hautement qualifié. Les couvents de Komodibi de Nyamina et de Bougouni,[75] les couvents Bokanana d'Amey, les centres de géomancie de Nionsonbougou, les centres occulistes de Labé, de Dia de Tombouctou, de Djenné ; Hamdallahix, Bandiagara et Guirir, ceux de Bossomnoré, Todjam, Bura-Saba, Yaté, Badinogo, Ramatoulaya, Barami, Duahubou, Marné, Sagbtenga, les centres magiques de Darsalami « pour l'acquisition par le rite infernal du poulet », des Airumba du Louroum « pour remédier à la stérilité des « sapeurs pompiers africains » — c'est-à-dire, « porteurs de vilains et vieux pantalons » du Bélédougou et du Mandé, les centres initiatiques pende, tshokwe, etc., bref, tout le continent est

75. The sanctuaries in Nyamina and Bougouni in Mali, traditionally known for its oral culture, were places where *Komodibi* (bards) would receive training and undergo rites of initiation. Other sites listed are elsewhere in Africa.

représenté. Dignement représente. L'on parle déjà du procès du siècle. « Le continent a été trahi, attaqué, il faut relever le défi. » « Il faut en finir une fois pour toutes. » « Il n'y a pas de continent appelé à diriger culturellement les autres. » « Nous estimons que c'est la culture bien comprise qui fait la dignité d'un peuple. » « Nous nous sentons aujourd'hui forts pour exporter la culture. » « Nous l'exportons déjà. » « Qu'on vienne encore nous parler de sauvagerie après les scènes d'anthropophagie d'Hitler !» « Nous n'avons pas de sous-culture. » « Culture à part entière ! » « Nous refusons de servir de cobayes aux ethnologues occidentaux. » « Nous ne sommes pas des curiosités préhistoriques ! » « Nous avons toujours eu foi en nous-mêmes. » « Pas de contre-culture en Afrique. » « La contre-culture est une monstruosité occidentale ; elle n'a rien à voir avec nous. » « Si l'Occident a perdu ses pédales, nous sommes prêts à lui apprendre à les redécouvrir. » « Nous ne sommes pas une société contre nature ni une société dénaturée ou une autre nature dénaturée. » « Ces notions ne seront pas autorisées à prendre racine en Afrique. » « Fini le temps où l'on nous prenait pour de purs objets d'une science universellement dénoncée comme pratique politique d'aliénation de l'homme. » « La science occidentale notamment sous sa forme ethnologique traduit son incapacité à rejoindre la subjectivité de ceux qu'on appelle abusivement les primitifs. » « Que des fils d'Afrique aient pu commettre de telles aberrations est inconcevable ! » « Le mépris affiché par ce chien égaré à l'endroit du continent est incommensurable. » « Est-il vraiment normal ? Ne faudrait-il pas le soumettre à un traitement rééquilibrant ? »

Ainsi s'expriment dans un grand brouhaha tous ces jeunes gens qui accompagnent les chefs des différents couvents. Élégamment vêtus, s'exprimant en un français impeccable. Tous formés dans des universités occidentales, les uns à Paris, à Londres, à Genève, à Bruxelles, les autres dans des universités américaines. Sont-ils techniciens bénévoles de la culture ou sont-ils incorporés dans ces lieux par un sort semblable au mien ? Question que je ne parviens pas à élucider. Ils paraissent, à en juger par leurs propos, convaincus de leur spécificité africaine comme les maîtres qu'ils servent. Ils paraissent tous aussi hostiles à ma cause. Formés à la dialectique occidentale, ils vont sans nul doute m'écraser par le poids de leurs arguments. Ils sont installés sur un terrain solide. Leur position est inattaquable. La mienne bâtie sur du sable mouvant résistera-t-elle à leurs assauts ? Jamais de ma vie je n'ai éprouvé l'impression de défaite de manière aussi cruelle. Ma carrière brillante dans le monde des savants m'apparaît aujourd'hui ridicule. Le Club de Rome auquel de plein droit j'appartiens me lâche. Mes hypothèses sur la réconciliation du public et de l'écrivain ; sur la rénovation de l'humanité par des valeurs autres que celles perçues par le rapport du Club ; mes hypothèses sur l'espace et le temps primordiaux, autant de points marqués qui m'ont hissé à un niveau jamais atteint par un Africain. Je revois en un éclair tous les Coopérants. Je ne suis plus qu'un souvenir à leurs yeux. L'existence humaine ! Qu'est-elle ? Un paquet de souvenirs, bons ou mauvais. Tous les génies subissent cette loi. Leur immortalité ? Un lien de souvenirs maintenu dans l'esprit des vivants. Qui suis-je dans leur esprit à cette heure ? Les longues diseussions avec la plupart d'entre eux se sont-elles déjà diluées dans l'oubli ? Les lumières qui émanaient de mon génie telles des lucioles éclairant le ciel ténébreux de ces Coopérants qui m'adoraient, j'ose à peine croire qu'elles n'ont connu qu'une existence éphémère ! J'ai misé sur eux ? Erreur de tactique ! Eux sont partis. Parmi mes « compatriotes », entre guillemets, je n'ai pas un seul « ami ». Si j'en avais un, je ne subirais pas la cruelle loi du silence. Silence complice, silence de démission ! Même pour Niaiseux qui expie en ce moment la fatalité de l'Histoire, je ne représente plus rien. Et la seule personne au monde avec qui je peux communier dans l'opacité des consciences est-elle en deuil ? Continue-t-elle la réclusion qui fut notre condition quotidienne ? Ma tendre épouse ! Le destin cruel qui s'abat sur moi s'acharne aussi contre elle. Le mur de l'incommunicabilité s'est installé plus épais, plus implacable. Me voilà pareil à cet être décrit par Robert Musil « qui ne peut ni parler ni être exprimé, qui disparaît sans voix dans la masse humaine, petit griffonnage sur les tables de l'Histoire, un être pareil à un flocon de neige égaré en plein été, suis-je réalité ou rêve, bon ou mauvais, précieux ou sans valeur ? ».[76] Inutile mon existence. Un poids stupide. Une pesanteur violente. Je ne rencontre qu'hostilité. Le sourire qu'on ne peut refuser à l'être humain contre quoi vais-je le marchander ? Rien ne peut illuminer mon visage. Solitude mon amante. On me refuse même le regard de mépris. Pourtant, tous ces jeunes sont autant que moi le produit des universités occidentales ! Un point nous rapproche : la culture ! Eux me haïssent. La haine, un trait de culture ! Non, fatalité de la nature entre eux et moi. C'est le seul dénominateur commun. J'ai choisi. Eux, non. Le choix est aux antipodes de la nature. Leurs contes, leurs fables, leurs légendes, leurs mythes, leurs épopées, ils appellent ça culture ! Contraintes pourtant de la nature. Un tas de déterminismes enlaçants, tordant le cou de l'individu pour l'obliger à regarder toujours le passé, à perpétuer ce dialogue avec les ancêtres. Disparus de notre univers, ceux-ci sont présents d'une présence transparente. Leur parole échappe à ce rôle réducteur

---

76. From Musil's autobiographical novella "Tonka" ("*Tonka*" 184).

que constitue l'écran de notre culture. La parole apparemment libre auraitelle un poids tel que le passage de ces techniciens dans les universités occidentales n'a laissé aucune trace en eux ? Pas même la possibilité du choix qui fonde l'acte de la culture ? La dialectique occidentale libère, celle de l'Africain contraint, enferme, asservit. A moins que, l'on ne sait par quelle habile ouverture au monde, la présence de ces jeunes soit une manière de sortir l'Afrique hors d'elle-même. Ce serait alors un coup génial digne de cette Afrique passée maîtresse de la symbolique ! Hypothèse peu probable pour des chefs écrasés sous le poids des fatalités d'une pensée entièrement asservissante. Un miracle se serait produit ici pour les ouvrir à la nécessité de se soumettre à la loi de ce que certains appellent dialogue des cultures ! Rôle, dans l'hypothèse, positif des techniciens.

Pendant que je déroule ces pensées, on achève le dispositif du procès. On semble y attacher une grande importance. Devant la chaise de chaque chef de délégation, est posé un escabeau, sculpté suivant des motifs propres à la provenance de celle-ci. Cependant, un même motif court d'un escabeau à l'autre : la présence du masque ici terrifiant, là menaçant. Les chaises, elles, sont aussi taillées de la même manière. Mais il s'y ajoute la présence de signes mystérieux qui semblent être une écriture particulière à ces couvents, car elle est très régulière.

Derrière, prennent place les conseillers techniques de la culture.

Quelques instants vont s'écouler encore avant l'entrée des chefs. Les techniciens s'animent, s'échangent des idées ; s'affairent. Des serviteurs mettent des guirlandes autour des masques suspendus aux quatre coins de la cour du procès. Des pieux supportent, tous les deux mètres, des crânes fixés au sommet. Dans son ensemble, le décor reste assez sobre.

Placé dans un coin de la scène, gardé par le gorille qui avait arrangé Niaiseux, j'observe le va-et-vient des serviteurs. La dernière main au décor est mise. Je m'attends d'un moment à l'autre à être placé au milieu de la scène comme un holocauste ou plutôt comme meneur de jeu. Je serai au centre du débat, d'un débat dont l'absurdité éclate d'une manière certaine : l'accusé est condamné à l'avance. De quoi m'accuse-t-on au juste ? Quelle est la compétence de la juridiction qui me met en jugement ?

— Chut ! Fait-on savoir à tous les conseillers de se taire car les chefs arrivent pour prendre place à la tribune. Ils entrent selon l'ordre réglé par la gérontocratie africaine. Tous ont un chasse-mouches. Des chapeaux faits entièrement en perles multicolores ornent leurs têtes. L'habillement tissé de raphia fin se compose essentiellement d'un pagne et d'une sorte de tunique sur laquelle est frappé l'écusson du couvent dont chacun est le chef.

Après un moment de recueillement debout, ils s'asseyent tous, les chefs. On fait signe à mon garde de corps de me pousser au centre de la scène. Je m'exécute sans attendre que la brute m'offre ses services. Un murmure sourd court dans l'assistance. Sans doute d'indignation. Un geste du chef du couvent accueillant suffit à rétablir le silence. Comme il convient, c'est à lui qu'il appartient d'exposer à ses pairs, après que le plus vieux ait ouvert la séance, les raisons de mon arrestation.

Traduction :

« Chers Camarades, vous avez tous eu les échos des derniers événements. Vous ne seriez pas ici aujourd'hui si quelque chose de grave ne s'était produit. Notre règlement organique nous interdit de mettre arbitrairement quiconque en état d'arrestation. Si cet énergumène comparaît devant vous, c'est parce que nous avons estimé que son crime dépasse toute proportion.

D'aucuns trouveront ce procès peut-être insolite. Dans le monde dit « libre », en effet, il n'en existe guère de ce genre. Un procès à base de délit culturel! Inconcevable. N'est-ce pas l'originalité de notre continent d'avoir échappé à ces compartimentages de la réalité : facteur politique, facteur économique, facteur culturel, facteur religieux, etc. La réalité est autrement complexe ; tout est imbriqué l'un dans l'autre. Le sacré est dans la célébration quotidienne de la vie. La coupure entre le profane et le sacré est ce crime dont le remords poursuit l'Occident nuit et jour. Remords à vrai dire rousseauiste qui pousse bon nombre d'intellectuels à venir, sous couleur de recherches scientifiques, s'emparer de nos rites, de nos mythes, de nos sacrifices pour retrouver une innocence et une enfance perdues. On apparente l'enfance au mythe du prétendu premier matin du monde. On s'ingénie à trouver ce milieu — « chaos primordial » —, de pur rythme, de pure durée, où le jour, paraît-il, qui se lève ne se distingue pas de la nuit qui tombe. On nous assimile à cette enfance, considérée comme le premier stade de l'humanité dans son évolution. Suivant cette logique de la confusion des genres et des contradictoires, l'athéisme ne s'oppose plus à l'incroyance ; ni le profane au sacré ; ni la haine à l'amour, ni le mépris à l'estime. C'est la nouvelle forme, subtile, d'exploitation forgée par l'Occident. Si l'on n'y prend garde, le bon Dieu lui-même s'y laisserait prendre et nous, nous nous retrouverons un beau matin au cœur de la subversion. Il sera trop tard quand nous nous en apercevrons. Le secret de notre vitalité, de notre pouvoir créateur se trouve dans nos rites et dans nos mythes. Qui apprivoise le secret de la culture d'un peuple, peut disposer de celui-ci à son gré. Il peut y introduire des éléments de désintégration ; peut asservir tout comme il peut promouvoir. Or l'Occident est arrivé aujourd'hui à percer le mécanisme secret de nos mythes ; réduits à un système d'opérations, ils sont étudiés algébriquement. Nous ne sommes plus que des abstractions, maniées par des symboles d'où notre subjectivité est complètement évacuée. Nous croyons avoir encore un discours mythique secret. Illusion. Nous ne nous appartenons plus. Nous sommes l'homme d'un autre. Les sceptiques parmi nous n'ont qu'à se rappeler comment, par l'apprivoisement de l'intimité de la matière, en réussissant à y introduire de la subversion par bombardements des particules, l'homme blanc a montré à Hiroshima ce dont il est capable. Il y est arrivé par une audace inouïe qui défie tout ; par de petits cambriolages perpétrés par chaque génération depuis des millénaires. Il ne lui a pas fallu cent ans pour percer le mystère de notre discours. Celui-ci est mis à nu. Disséqué, les morceaux parqués dans des concepts qui sont une mystérieuse algèbre, connue seulement de quelques initiés. Ses lois de fonctionnement parfaitement maîtrisées. Plus aucun contour ni recoin ne leur échappe.

Mais il existe cependant un domaine où nous sommes encore maîtres de notre discours, où nous pouvons nous réfugier sans être inquiétés. C'est tout le poids de notre subjectivité incarné admirablement par le conteur: l'espace-temps intranscriptible et intraduisible ; la liberté d'évolution, le dramatique du geste, du mot, des modulations, des appels, des demandes, des interpellations, de l'imaginaire articulé par le corps à corps du dialogue, de la présence de l'Autre. Tout un royaume tabou. Interdit. Mais richesse infinie. Kaléidoscope d'une infinitude de langages. Voyez le conteur imiter le langage du léopard, du lion, du lièvre, du renard, de la vieille sorcière, de l'enfant. Dédoublement, redoublement, déguisement, travestissement, imitation, copie, expressivité sont cet univers qu'on voudrait aujourd'hui dynamiter, livrer à l'étranger. Une main criminelle s'apprêtait à s'abattre sur nous. Mais nous sommes intervenus à temps. Elle est hors d'état de nuire. Et pour longtemps. J'ai nommé ce Chien d'étranger que voici. Sorti de notre terre, je n'ose pas dire de notre race, il n'a d'africain que la peau qu'il troquerait volontiers à la première occasion. Par choix froidement réfléchi il nous a tourné le dos avec mépris. Il ne croit pas au dialogue des cultures. Il s'est emmuré dans une forteresse inexpugnable : la solitude hautaine et agressive. Jour et nuit nous l'avons filé. De lui-même, dans un mouvement de provocation criminelle, il est venu à nous. Écoutez, chers Camarades : cherchant à fonder une nouvelle écriture, au lieu d'utiliser des armes de sa « culture », pour accoucher de son discours, il s'est tourné vers l'Afrique. Oh! Sacrilège ! Nos rites d'initiation et magiques! Cet athée a osé attenter au sacré lui qui fait profession d'incroyant. Notre culture ne l'intéresse que pour servir ses ambitions. Traître ! C'est le baiser de Judas renouvelé.[77]

Davantage. Par son écriture gestuelle, c'est notre dernier refuge qu'il voulait livrer à l'ennemi. C'est nous, c'est nos enfants, c'est nos femmes qu'il trahissait. Geste suprêmement négrier. Notre secret vendu, on allait disposer de nous à leur guise. Notre intimité violée et désacralisée, nous allions devenir des prostituées. Qui d'entre nous resterait insensible devant de tels crimes ?

---

77. The speaker evokes the kiss of betrayal by which Judas identifies Jesus to the crowd that comes to seize him in the Garden of Gethsemane (Matt. 26.47–50).

Nous avons toujours cultivé l'amitié entre les peuples. Le geste de ce Chien tendait à poser des germes de guerre et en Occident sa nouvelle patrie et chez nous en Afrique. Chez nous, il arrachait notre nudité, notre espace pour les livrer tels des esclaves à leur discours écrit. Avec eux, le destinataire, le sujet et l'imaginaire de notre parole prenaient tout droit également le chemin de l'esclavage. Judas des Temps modernes, te rends-tu compte de l'énormité de ton crime ?

Plus grave. En Occident l'expérience artistique pour être authentique passe par ce qu'ils appellent le dérèglement méthodique de tous les sens[78] *; par l'expérience du gouffre insondable, du totalement autre. En venant chez nous tu avais assimilé nos rites à ces séances de dérèglement des sens ! Comment as-tu osé mettre en parallèle nos rites avec tous les vices auxquels se livrent vos artistes occidentaux : la drogue, la marijuana, le haschich, l'alcool, les vices contre nature ? Il était parfaitement de ton droit de te faire vicieux, maudit, autoérotique mais — et c'est là que le bât blesse — tu dépassais les limites de ce droit quand par une intention perverse tu dénaturais nos cérémonies sacrificielles malgré les prémonitions des ancêtres.*

En Occident même ces armes miraculeuses allaient être reçues comme des boulets lancés par des canons nègres. Nous serions passés pour des irresponsables! Qui prendrait la res-

78. Echoing Rimbaud, who declared in 1871 that "le Poète se fait *voyant* par un long, immense et raisonné *dérèglement* de *tous les sens* (*Œuvres* 251).

ponsabilité d'une telle guerre ? Nos armes allaient désintégrer leur écriture, devenue caisse de résonance pour toutes les révolutions idéologiques ; enfer concentrationnaire où le flux et le reflux de la pensée dépouillent régulièrement de leur aura dogmatique toutes les idéologies ; mise en accusation perpétuelle de toute écriture antérieure.

Vous conviendrez avec moi, chers Camarades, qu'il ne nous appartenait pas de livrer nos secrets à ce Chien d'étranger pour envenimer en Occident ce qui constitue tendance latente à la subversion. Nous cultivons l'amitié comme nos ancêtres l'ont toujours fait. La philosophie africaine interdit de nous livrer à la provocation. C'est pourquoi, je considère cet Étranger comme un irresponsable. De ce fait, il devrait subir un châtiment exemplaire ; j'ai parlé. »

Pendant tout ce réquisitoire qui se termine dans les bonnes traditions des ministères publics, j'écoute attentivement et observe les réactions des conseillers. Elles sont dans l'ensemble d'approbation. Quelques minutes de répit. Les chefs et les conseillers se consultent et se concertent. L'éloquence du chef de la place et de son technicien est persuasive.

La séance reprend. La parole est donnée directement à un autre conseiller.

« Camarade, vous avez bien parlé. L'Afrique a été insultée. L'offense sans mesure demande réparation. Cependant nous ne dissimulons pas le retentissement qu'aura ce procès sans

précédent, notamment son verdict en Afrique même et dans le monde. Le crime de trahison, le sacrilège, la tentative athée de vouloir s'approprier et livrer a l'ennemi nos secrets les plus intimes et notre patrimoine le plus sacré appellent une répression. C'est un devoir et un droit inaliénable pour l'Afrique de défendre son patrimoine culturel. Elle a été par le passé pillée. Voyez le British Museum ! Quel scandale ! Pillage systématique de l'Égypte ancienne. Le Louvre ! Tervueren ![79] Ce vandalisme qui caractérise les premiers contacts de l'Occident et de l'Afrique, il ne faut pas qu'il se répète. L'Afrique vidée de ses richesses constituera toujours l'un des crimes qui pèse sur la conscience de l'Europe. Nous admettons encore qu'on pompe nos matières premières, nos œuvres d'art. Qu'on vienne toucher notre subjectivité, pour nous faire passer de l'ordre subjectif à l'ordre objectif, voilà qui nous irrite ! Nous disons halte, coquin ! Après nous avoir réduits en esclavage, après nous avoir dépersonnalisés, non contents de la domination installée en plein cœur du continent, ils portent aujourd'hui la violence sur notre discours. Le développement linéaire et orienté de nos récits, on veut le soumettre à leurs programmes narratifs. Violence d'enchaînements logiques, violence téléologique exercée avec désinvolture par des sémanticiens sans scrupule ! Violence d'une vivisection sauvage de nos récits. Violence d'une symboli-

79. Belgium's Royal Museum for Central Africa, established in 1897 to showcase King Leopold's possessions and to advertise the king's "civilizing mission" in the Congo.

sation brutale où nos réalités sont entièrement déshumanisées. Assisterons-nous éternellement cois en face de cette forme de vandalisme ? De cet ethnocentrisme déprimant, exploitant, débilitant, dévirilisant ? Notre discours introduit brutalement dans le leur n'est plus conscience de quelque chose mais regardé comme conscience de relations pures. Nous aurions volontiers admis une assomption de notre parole par leur subjectivité. Non, arrachés de la nôtre sans façon et ménagement, nous sommes objectivés dans un jeu de relations conceptuelles. L'articulation socio-culturelle évacuée et avec elle toute l'expérience accumulée par des générations et des générations, la corde au cou, c'est la voie de l'esclavage que nous perpétuons. Bras croisés ? Non, Camarades, agissons ! »

Un troisième conseiller :

« Camarades, l'Occident et, avec lui, tous ses fils spirituels sont à la croisée des chemins. Ils sont à la recherche de remaniements culturels. Je me pose la question pourquoi le prix à payer est-il celui de l'assujettissement de l'Autre ? La tentative de ce Chien aurait pu être un cas intéressant de dialogue des cultures. Mais le problème mal posé au départ nous a lancés dans une voie sans issue. Quel que soit le verdict de ce procès, l'Assemblée doit éviter de donner à croire au monde que l'Afrique se refuse à tout dialogue. Notre procès porte moins sur le fait de savoir si le discours occidental peut se nourrir du discours africain que sur les procédés d'asservissement et de viol de celui-ci. Le problème de dialogue, de symbiose entre discours

relevant de cultures hétérogènes reste posé sur le plan des principes. Ceux-ci nous échappent. Nous n'avons aucune prise sur eux. Dans cet ordre d'idées, cet aliéné, traduit aujourd'hui devant nous, reste dans ses droits les plus sacrés. Libre à lui de poser que le discours imaginaire qui hante ses nuits — le roman — peut être dans une situation d'osmose avec l'imaginaire africain — le récit. Son credo lui commande de croire que le roman peut se dérouler selon un mouvement pouvant épouser les voies des récits de chez nous. Naïveté ? Audace ? Cela nous importe peu. Nous devons nous cantonner dans ce que nous croyons être un délit. »

Des mouvements divers se dessinent parmi les conseillers. Approbation chez certains, désapprobation chez d'autres. Plusieurs demandent la parole. Le débat semble se circonscrire autour des procédés qui m'avaient conduit à la tentative d'apprivoisement de leur discours. Le principe d'osmose entre discours ne semble pas les intéresser. Ils se rendent compte qu'il y a risque à s'aventurer dans une voie dont l'issue n'est pas certaine. Emboîter en effet un discours pris dans une culture différente dans un autre dont le suc est constitué de thèmes, de symboles, de mythes spécifiques, paraît une gageure. Il faut en montrer la possibilité théorique, la fonder sur des bases sérieuses. Établir la subsomption dans la nouvelle structure, les effets fécondants dans celle-ci. Des cultures, c'est des nappes d'images, des symboles structurants, des systèmes de représentations. Réussira-t-on à en montrer scientifiquement la possibilité de communication inter-lacustre ? Des sous-sols étanches, imperméables ? Des vases communicants ?[80] Quel artiste peut prétendre puiser à cette profondeur souterraine ? Communier à des nappes d'eau hétérogènes mais également revigorantes ? Illusion ? Des vrais artistes creusent jusqu'à cette couche. Ceux qui n'y peuvent atteindre sont pareils à ces mandragores desséchées faute de limon fécondant. Les racines fourchues, l'arbre s'aggrippe à des sédiments superficiels, trompeurs qui recouvrent des formations virilisantes.

Le discours imaginaire pousse ses racines dans le discours de la vie sociale, projetée dans les fantaisies, les rêves, les désirs des hommes ; dans des mondes possibles. L'écriture est évocation de ces fictions. Imaginer qu'elle puisse s'abreuver à des profondeurs du discours social d'un autre peuple, l'apprivoiser comme « on emboîte Autre dans structure » paraît être un crime de présomption. C'est la raison pour laquelle ils n'osent s'aventurer sur un terrain aussi glissant.

---

80. In *Les vases communicants* (1932), André Breton argued that society could be revolutionized by uniting into a coherent and organic whole the "communicating vessels" of everyday reality and the world of dreams.

Un autre conseiller, impatient, prend la parole.

« *Camarades, nous vous avons entendu discourir. Les uns et les autres ont dit de fort belles choses. J'aimerais poser une question fondamentale. Avons-nous le droit d'instituer ce procès ? Sur quelle base pouvons-nous arrêter un individu, le juger sur le chef de l'athéisme ? La solidité de l'argumentation repose là-dessus. Un fils du pays, aliéné, prétend avoir coupé le cordon ombilical qui le reliait à sa mère l'Afrique. C'est un renégat, bien sûr ! Monstrueux ! Mais cela nous autorise-t-il à le juger ! J'aimerais qu'on me réponde ?* »

Un conseiller de l'Ouest-Africain :

« *Crois-tu que nous nous serions déplacés sans une raison sérieuse et grave ? Le procès que nous instituons serait-il donc arbitraire ? Serais-tu vendu et aliéné ? Camarades, il y a lieu de resserrer nos coudes. Nous commençons à dévier. Peut-être serait-il souhaitable que nous rappelions quelques principes élémentaires du droit des peuples et des nations. Chaque peuple a droit à la sécurité interne et externe. Toutes mesures tendant à assurer cette double sécurité sont non seulement moralement permises mais s'imposent obligatoirement. Aucune nation ne peut s'y soustraire. Elles peuvent être préventives, car mieux vaut prévenir que guérir. Le droit des peuples et des nations le reconnaît.*

En ce qui concerne notre procès, notre sécurité a-t-elle été menacée ? A l'extérieur comme à l'intérieur ? Si la réponse à ces questions est affirmative nous avons le fondement juridique solide que nous cherchons. Je défie quiconque de me contredire. »

Un conseiller de l'Afrique centrale :

« Les questions telles que formulées par notre camarade ouest-africain me paraissent pertinentes et suffisamment circonscrites pour que notre débat ait un fondement juridique inattaquable.

Notre sécurité a-t-elle été menacée ? Oui ! A-t-elle été effectivement attaquée tant de l'extérieur que de l'intérieur ? Oui ! »

Un oui massif ponctue çà et là ces propos dans l'Assemblée. Le dernier orateur semble avoir tiré d'embarras ces jeunes universitaires qui s'embourbaient dans des méandres et dans une spirale semblables à ces zigzags dessinés par des enfants. Le procès s'acheminerait-il vers son dénouement ?

« Je demande que sans tarder soit rendu le verdict. Tous ceux qui attentent à la sécurité d'un état savent ce qui les attend. Qu'un juste châtiment soit infligé à cet énergumène. »

Le plus jeune des conseillers éclatant d'indignation :

— *« Camarades, dit-il, j'ai écouté avec intérêt tous les orateurs. »*

— *« Il ne manquerait plus que cela »*, riposte une voix tonitruante dans l'Assemblée.

— *« J'ai été frappé, reprend le jeune conseiller, par la justesse des propos des uns et des autres. Chaque orateur a apporté sa contribution à la clarification de ce débat qui aurait pu sombrer dans la pire des confusions. Mais le génie africain, celui de nos ancêtres veille hélas ! et nous a évité la honte universelle. Je me demande cependant s'il est vraiment temps de prononcer un verdict quelconque. Avons-nous épuisé le sujet, retourné les arguments sept fois ou comme le disent les Warega "fait deux pas, trois pas" ?*[81] *Toute précipitation serait préjudiciable aussi bien à la cause du criminel qu'à la nôtre. J'ai toujours horreur du terrorisme, qu'il provienne de quelque forme d'intolérance que du fascisme le plus terre à terre. Il est plus dangereux quand il est intellectuel. Le salut de l'Afrique n'est pas dans l'abdication de soi-même au bénéfice du conformisme. En instituant ce procès notre intention n'est pas de dresser une muraille de Chine autour du continent pour empêcher les intellectuels de dialoguer avec leurs collègues d'ailleurs. Le plus grand malheur qui s'annonce pour l'Afrique c'est la nouvelle idéologie incarnée un peu partout par la recherche d'un certain unanimisme.* Idem velle, idem nolle.[82] *Le pluralisme est devenu crime. Je me pose la question : régression ou progrès ? Depuis les temps les plus reculés, notre continent, replié par des contraintes et des fatalités historiques dans un narcissisme collectif, ne nous a entretenus que par des bavardages gratuits dans lesquels nous nous sommes complus dans une image spéculaire de*

---

81. The Warega are a Congolese ethnic group.
82. "Same desires, same dislikes," an old Roman adage.

nous-mêmes. Notre discours n'est jamais parvenu à se libérer des contraintes de la pensée mythique, stade suprême de l'unanimisme. Nous nous sommes nourris de celui-ci depuis toujours. Unanimité autour d'un système dogmatique où l'esprit critique et le pluralisme d'opinions étaient inexistants. Notre attitude aujourd'hui face à ce jeune n'est-elle pas celle d'une amante jalouse de son mâle ? de son trésor qu'elle n'ose exposer de peur de voir d'autres le ravir.

Qu'on me comprenne bien. Loin de moi d'approuver tout ce que ce jeune homme a fait. Mais je voudrais attirer notre attention sur une idéologie courante, l'idéologie africaniste qui veut que les réalités africaines soient spécifiques, originales. Ce qu'un camarade appelait tout à l'heure "attentat contre notre sécurité" n'est rien d'autre que "attentat contre notre spécificité", contre notre repli sur nous-mêmes. Mais n'oublions pas qu'une "spécificité" prépare sa propre asphyxie dans la mesure où elle ne reçoit pas d'oxygène de l'extérieur. Les cultures ne survivent que par l'ouverture à d'autres cultures qui les libèrent de leur tendance au narcissisme collectif. La tentative de notre accusé est-elle si condamnable ? Ne faudrait-il pas y voir l'audace d'un jeune chercheur qui a tenté de libérer notre discours de ses infirmités en l'ouvrant à un discours plus théorique, plus universel. Si son auteur avait abouti n'aurait-il pas fondé une théorie révolutionnaire du roman ? Quel enrichissement pour nous et pour l'Occident ? Pour l'humanité ? Une science nouvelle de l'écriture dont le fondateur aurait été un Nègre ? Qui aurait été insensible ? L'Occident a eu son Marx, son Freud; l'Afrique n'en a pas encore. Demeurerons-nous éternellement suiveurs des autres ? A la face du monde nous n'avons été capables d'exhiber que des percussions rythmiques, élevées aujourd'hui par certaines nations africaines au rang de spécificité nègre. A longueur de journée des masses hébétées s'adonnent à des séances de déhanchement : redécouverte de la rythmicité primitive que la colonisation avait mise en veilleuse. Le problème posé par ce procès est donc d'importance. Ou nous consacrerons la régression de l'Afrique ou nous ouvrirons notre continent au progrès. »

Ce discours si percutant ne semble pas beaucoup émouvoir. La majorité des visages ne cachaient pas leur désapprobation.

« Camarade brillant universitaire, ton discours séduit. Mais tu recules le problème. Car enfin il s'agit précisément de savoir si l'ouverture du discours africain à un autre modèle plus théorique et plus universel constitue une atteinte à la sécurité intérieure et extérieure du continent et, de ce fait, mérite un châtiment exemplaire. Y a-t-il eu agression ou à tout le moins tentative d'agression ? Tout est là. Ne divaguons plus. Serrons de très près l'argumentation. »

Cette dernière intervention semble amener plus de confusion dans le débat. Les esprits commencent à s'échauffer. Ceux qui, pressés, avaient cru le problème résolu d'un trait de parole, ne semblaient plus aussi affirmatifs qu'au début. La discussion, bien qu'ayant atteint un haut niveau de tenue, tombe dans l'impasse. Tous les jeunes conseillers tiennent à prendre la parole, plus par désir de faire montre de ce qu'ils avaient appris dans les différentes universités occidentales que par souci de faire avancer le procès. Après chaque intervention on a l'impression qu'on s'enfonce dans le byzantinisme. Comment débrouiller ? Le procès n'est plus celui de Giambatista mais un affrontement des conseillers-techniciens dont les joutes oratoires n'ont de positif que le fait qu'elles n'ont pas encore réussi à dégénérer en rixes.

Les chefs des délégations, eux, apparemment ne semblent rien comprendre à ces discours des jeunes. On les avait fait venir pour juger un traître, un blasphémateur, un athée qui, poussé par une audace criminelle, avait porté la main sur leurs rites les plus sacrés. C'est cela qu'il faut juger. Beaucoup commencent à s'impatienter des arguties souvent pédantes et exhibitionnistes des conseillers.

D'un geste impérieux, le plus vieux des chefs obtient le silence.

— A-t-on donné au traître la potion de vérité avant l'ouverture de ce procès, s'enquiert-il ?

— Non, répondent en chœur ceux du couvent accueillant.

— Comment avez-vous pu négliger un rite aussi essentiel dans un procès ? Les jeunes s'exhibent ; personne ne pense à interroger le prévenu ?

A cet instant précis tout le monde se tourne vers moi. Je lis dans les yeux des chefs comme une sensation de satisfaction provoquée par l'impuissance des jeunes intellectuels à trancher une palabre. Pendant toute la joute oratoire, ils ne disaient rien ; observaient ; ricanaient sous leur barbe.

— Qu'on m'apporte un bouc et le vase des potions.

On fait avancer l'animal. D'un seul coup d'épée, la tête est séparée et deux hommes se précipitent avec le vase pour recueillir le sang. Un silence impressionnant s'abat sur l'Assemblée.

Le mélange de sang frais et du liquide qu'on venait d'apporter constitue la potion des solennités dans les couvents. On s'en sert exceptionnellement. Dans mon cas, les choses sont claires : le chef d'accusation ne laisse pas de doute sur sa gravité.

Un frisson me parcourt de la tête aux pieds. Et, à l'instant, un vers de Michel Leiris monte des profondeurs de mon cœur :

« La pieuvre gonfle ses bras de sang
Cinq tentacules, cinq bras d'acier… »[83]

---

83. From the surrealist poet and ethnographer Michel Leiris's "Le chasseur de têtes" (*Haut mal* 44; 43–45), in which an African headhunter sees octopi as floating severed heads.

Image de l'humanité primitive qui se meurt dans l'univers de meurtre et de destruction ; des terreurs et d'effroi ; de l'érotisation du sang, de la peur et des horreurs.

Le bouc immolé est censé mettre l'assistance en relation magique avec l'être à sacrifier dans l'espoir d'une libération de la vérité et d'une réussite. L'on tue en moi Giambatista pour que renaisse le Nègre. Le mélange du sang du bouc et du mien par ce rite masochiste et sadique rendra plus authentiques les rapports entre eux et moi. Du moins ils le croient. Une preuve et une épreuve : un nouvel homme. L'enchaînement pour toujours de ma réussite possible dans l'art romanesque. La mort du discours occidental : de cette transcription gestuelle de mon expérience directe intérieure telle que je l'ai voulue inspirée de l'oralité, mariée dans une union dynamique avec l'écriture. L'Afrique a eu finalement raison. Et cependant rien de vrai !

On me fait monter au milieu sur un escabeau. La potion fait son œuvre. Les jambes lourdes et comme aimantées me retiennent solidement. On me lie les mains derrière le dos. Cependant aucune violence physique n'est exercée sur moi. La pluie d'injures qu'ils avaient l'habitude de verser sur leur victime semble avoir cessé. C'est qu'ils sont sûrs maintenant que je suis des leurs. Point de mire de tous les regards, dans cette arène publique et ouverte, je suis pareil à ces victimes chrétiennes que les Romains livraient aux lions. Quel plaisir sadique rechercheraient-ils ? La poursuite de leur vérité demande-t-elle d'aller « jusqu'au sang, sachant que la fustigation est excellente pour affermir les chairs » ?[84] N'est-il pas trop facile de cueillir une victime non séduite ? Abattu, telle une prostituée qui se livre, quel motif de conquête puis-je encore leur offrir ? Le discours tué, la parole instantanée reprend vie en moi et me restitue à leur univers ; univers de l'immédiat, de l'hésitant, du fugace, des associations spontanées, inconscientes ; univers du non-retour en arrière. J'échangeais la Galaxie Gutenberg contre une imagerie fugace du monde.[85] Je me plongeais dans un fleuve sans rivages où il m'était interdit de me baigner deux fois. Je retrouvais les mimiques jubilatoires qu'offre la parole au primitif dans la présence de soi à soi. Abandon de soi ; refus de conquête ; démission de soi.

Pourquoi cette obstination à m'offrir en victime ? Cet entêtement ? Resterait-il encore un instinct à assouvir ? A présent tout est joué. Je n'ai plus de soupir à pousser. J'ai eu mon printemps et mon été. A l'arrivée de l'automne

---

84. A quotation from Leiris's hallucinatory novel *Aurora* (87), from a scene in which a temple priest abuses his female slaves.

85. In *The Gutenberg Galaxy* (1962), Marshall McLuhan analyzed the impact of the mass media on "typographic man."

l'été a fui. Vaincu, exfolié, dévêtu de l'habit de lumière de l'été, je ne suis plus qu'une étoile éteinte précocement.

Que puis-je leur opposer ? Ma faiblesse ? Absurdité ! Indifférence ? Étranger à eux, je le suis ! A présent ma défaite est leur victoire. L'espoir de me ramener à eux est une semence. Fin étrangement écho de ma carrière qui, en ses débuts, avait résonné du cri de l'échec.

— Jeune homme, m'interpelle le chef, un proverbe de chez nous dit : « La fougère amère n'est mangée que par un étranger. » Et un autre : « Celui qui se trouvait dans le giron de l'épervier ne s'est pas brûlé, mais celui qui se trouvait sur son dos s'est brûlé. » Je ne connais pas vos théories sur l'art de juger. Mais nous avons une sagesse égale si pas supérieure, transmise de génération en génération, à celle que les Blancs vous ont apprise. Grâce à elle nos sociétés connaissent un équilibre interne. Nous n'avons rien à regretter ni à rechercher ailleurs dans ce domaine précis. Sachez cependant qu'un animal n'oublie pas ses traces. Vous avez voulu nous faire croire que vous n'étiez plus des nôtres. Vous nous avez dérangés de jour et de nuit tout en faisant profession de renégat. Vous ne le faisiez pas en aveugle. Vous vous êtes emparé sciemment de nos rites. Vous saviez ce qui vous attendait. Des avertissements sibyllins et sévères vous avaient été en effet signifiés. Un proverbe nous enseigne : « S'il n'y a pas de poissons dans l'étang, ne laisse pas tes enfants se tuer par des moustiques. » C'est pourquoi « une tortue qui tombe dans un trou a beau se débattre, elle n'en sortira pas ». Écoutez bien :

— Êtes-vous pardonnable ?

— ...

— Vous ne répondez pas ! Un de vos proverbes dit : « Un homme averti en vaut deux. » Quand vous vous êtes adressé à nous pour devenir grand écrivain, pour égaler les Blancs, ignoriez-vous le risque que vous couriez ? Vous savez bien que « si vous vous liez d'amitié avec une abeille, approvisionnez-vous en palmiers car elle aime le vin de palme » !

— ...

— Vous ne répondez pas ! Pour vous nous étions morts. Pourquoi reveniez-vous troubler nos sommeils ? Ne saviez-vous pas que « l'argent emprunté, on ne l'utilise jamais pour enterrer un mort » ? Et « le cadavre d'un endetté s'enterre de bonne heure pour éviter les créanciers ».

— ...

— Vous ne répondez pas ![86] C'est parce que je vous parle en proverbes ! Pourtant c'est le lait premier qui vous

86. At his trial before Pontius Pilate, Jesus refused three times to answer charges against him (Matt. 27).

avait nourri, qui avait meublé votre esprit ! « Se souvenir est un signe de sagesse, oublier signe d'idiotie. » « Quand on va trop vite on finit par dépasser la bifurcation. » C'est votre cas. Vous êtes aujourd'hui entre nos mains. Nous ne vous laisserons pas partir. Vous serez condamné à l'opération « retour au pays natal ».[87] Vous passerez le restant de vos jours parmi nous ? Vous connaîtrez tour à tour les joies d'habiter aujourd'hui ici, aujourd'hui là-bas. Jusqu'à ce que vous ayez fait le tour de tous les couvents quatre-vingt-sept fois quatre-vingt-sept fois.

Applaudissements nourris. « La sagesse a parlé », clame-t-on d'un peu partout. « Il a été incapable de dire un seul mot contre le réquisitoire. » « La sagesse africaine l'a emporté face à la prétendue rhétorique occidentale dont il se gargarisait. » « Lui qui quitte notre culture pour en embrasser une autre soi-disant plus authentique a été incapable de saisir un mot au langage natal, comment serait-il capable de pénétrer la profondeur du langage des Blancs qui, eux, ne se baignent pas dans la même eau que nous ?» « C'est un mystificateur. » « Il ne mérite que cela. » « C'est bien et c'est bien dit. » « L'imposture a été démasquée. »

— « Si tu poursuis des collines, reprend le chef, tu dormiras en brousse, si tu te mets à contempler de belles

87. Citing Césaire's *Cahier d'un retour au pays natal* (1939), in which the poet envisioned a hallucinatory return from Paris to his homeland of Martinique.

femmes tes yeux seront fatigués. Tu es l'alouette qui a découvert la fourmi ailée, mais celle-ci échoit aux gens qui ont de gros ventres. » Ainsi donc vous faudra-t-il vous mettre à l'école de la sagesse. Vous êtes pareil à cet israélite qui après deux mille ans d'errance retrouve la terre de Sion. Le suc de la terre désertée est beaucoup trop riche pour accueillir l'enfant prodigue. »

Tonnerre d'applaudissements. Des cris hystériques fusent de toutes les bouches. Foule en délire. Joyeuse parturition. Éternelle Afrique ! La communion du groupe semble se souder plus dans le verbe que dans l'action véritable. C'est pourquoi bon nombre de nations africaines sont entraînées dans des délires de métamorphoses verbales pompeusement baptisées de révolutions ! Le verbe ! Leur gibecière magique.

— « La parole vient d'un homme tout comme la plume vient de l'oiseau. Le silence est la prison de la parole. Celle-ci peut se libérer si elle se réfugie dans le soupir. »

— « C'est percutant ! » « C'est le dernier clou ! » « Une leçon d'écriture jamais vue !» « De mémoire d'homme, on n'a vu administrer pareille leçon ! »

— « Le manioc qu'on grille à jeun pousse à raviver le feu sans interruption ! »

Le chef est continuellement interrompu par des vivats bruyants. Chacune de ses phrases est ponctuée par des battements de mains frénétiques. On a l'impression qu'il libère littéralement son monde d'un malheur eschatologique et d'un refoulement collectif.

Depuis le début du procès je n'ai pas proféré un seul mot. Mon silence est interprété comme une défaite. Mieux : comme une désaliénation et une conversion. Le silence est d'or, la parole trop riche en espérance, traîtresse.

Je suis donc un condamné. Un rejeté. Tiré d'une société et jeté dans une autre ! Quel sort réel ? Réintégration ou éternel bannissement ? Toute condamnation n'est-elle pas un rejet de la société des humains ? Ils ont cru me récupérer mais, en fait, ne m'ont-ils pas perdu définitivement ? J'ai quitté un cachot pour en occuper un autre plus ouvert, aux dimensions de l'Afrique. J'avais écouté ma sentence sans manifester le moindre sentiment. Personne ne m'observait. Le délire provoqué par les paroles du chef me soustrayait de leur monde le temps de leurs éclats de rire. Puis une fois l'euphorie passée, leurs regards me replongeaient dans le cachot. Je m'étais interdit de manifester ne fût-ce qu'un hochement de tête. Laisser transparaître un sentiment quelconque eût été donner un signe d'espérance. Je refusais d'être complice de moi-même. Révolte, indifférence sont des semences d'espoir. Or j'étais, depuis mon arrestation, condamné.

Pas une plage de soleil n'apparaissait à mon horizon. Les « miens » m'arrachaient à « mon monde » pour me jeter dans la prison de l'éternité. Mon crime c'est d'avoir été coupé de leur communion. Tout leur appareil judiciaire n'aura été qu'une mise en scène d'un réflecteur où j'avais pu lire ma condition ; notre condition. Regard narcissique. Image spéculaire. Partage de l'ironie et de la crispation amèrement jubilatoire. Crime ? N'est-ce pas celui de toute l'humanité ! Du regard refusé. Du cillement d'yeux. Du désir non réalisé. Du refoulement. De l'art. De l'imprévisible de la création. De l'écriture, mélange de pensées, de rêves, de fantaisie, d'attentes, coulé dans une « somme de la méditation et de l'expression » selon le mot juste de Bachelard.[88] Maîtres de la dramatisation, ils ont assouvi leur soif du crime en allant jusqu'au bout de leurs désirs. J'étais la victime tout indiquée. Ils avaient cru me voir tomber dans le piège de la révolte et de la pitié. Ils ne méritaient pas ce régal facile. C'eut été leur donner une chance de se reconnaître en moi, de reconnaître un frère. Le bourreau n'a droit à aucune lueur de l'aube. Il se coupe lui-même du regard réconciliant. La justice humaine, une machine implacable, crapuleuse. Danse macabre. Partouze indéfendable. Épitomé de l'his-

---

88. Citing Gaston Bachelard's definition of "l'homme littéraire" in the writer's 1943 essay on the imagination, *L'air et les songes* (302).

toire humaine. Eux, acteurs ? A vrai dire spectateurs. Je leur offrais de pouvoir lire leur condition. L'abîme qui me séparait d'eux est celui-là même qui rendait chacun d'eux étranger aux autres dans l'Assemblée. Mon spectacle loin de les unir les a éloignés encore davantage les uns des autres et du reste du genre humain. La solidarité proverbiale de l'Afrique n'est qu'un opium de désunion. J'ai paru souder leur communion. Mais ma condamnation ne scellait-elle pas ce pacte de l'opacité qui colle à la condition humaine ?

Condamné à l'errance, moi, GIAMBATISTA ! Pourquoi ont-ils mené à moitié leur dessein criminel ? Une exécution capitale n'eut-elle pas mieux valu ? De couvent à couvent, c'est autant dire d'oubli en oubli ! Un couvent à peine quitté pour un autre me couvrira aussitôt de l'horizon de l'oubli. De l'obscurité médiévale et millénaire de l'Afrique. De cette auréole du continent noir qui dissout les personnalités dans l'anonymat. Retour à ce temps ténébreux de l'espace sauvage. Me voilà marginalisé ! Noyé dans une sorte de fog polluant, Tous ceux qui m'ont condamné, pollueurs ! Les paroles du vieux chef qui déclenchaient du délire ne ressembaient-elles pas à ces nuages de fumée qui polluent nos grandes villes ? Ordures, immondices ! Dire qu'ils se sont régalés devant mon spectacle comme l'on boit du rhum antillais ! Comment sortir l'Afrique de cet épais brouillard de l'ensauvagement ? Recroquevillée sur elle-même comme une feuille de papier à la chaleur, elle est aujourd'hui menée par quelques mythes qui nous laissent rêveurs ! Les peuples à peine éveillés se laissent conduire tels des agneaux sacrifiés à l'autel des dieux. Immolés aux autels de la Révolution, de la Démocratie, réalités pourtant impalpables sous le ciel des monarques féodaux qui pullulent dans le continent ! Inflation verbale, délire de mots, nouvelle sauce appelée à assaisonner la politique africaine. Les masses hagardes plongées dans des hallucinations diurnes collectives. Socialisme, Voie africaine, Révolution constituent des échafauds sur lesquels on les immole ; leur guillotine le sous-développement. Condamnées elles aussi par un mécanisme implacable ! Pénalisées par le dieu capital. Marginalisation ! Périphérie ! Euphémismes cruels ! La vérité : l'échange inégal, nouvelle forme de la tragédie. Les dieux, vaincus par la bêtise humaine, se sont tus. Les masses sont conduites à l'abattoir sans avoir été jugées. Une poignée de bourreaux les assassinent tous les jours à petit feu. Stop ! Halte-là, tas de misérables criminels ! Vous avez nom : privilégiés ! Jusques à quand subirons-nous les contraintes de votre mythologie. ASSEZ DE SCANDALE ![89]

---

89. A quotation from Césaire's *Cahier d'un retour au pays natal* (32), in which Césaire protested against the exploitation of the Caribbean, including native women, by white colonists.

Ce dernier cri que j'avais cru purement obsessionnel avait, en fait, débordé mon discours interne. Je m'étais réveillé en sursaut de mes fantasmes. Je me frottai les yeux instinctivement, réajustai mes lunettes, respirai un bon coup. Je jetai un regard autour de moi. J'étais seul. Seul. L'Assemblée s'était dispersée. Je ne m'en étais pas rendu compte. Seul au milieu de la scène ! Depuis combien de temps ? Allaient-ils revenir pour continuer le procès ? Leur départ serait-il une sorte de renvoi en délibéré ? A huitaine peut-être ? Ma condamnation ne serait-elle donc pas encore intervenue ? Non, c'est une vision occidentale des choses !

Eux tiennent à marquer leur spécificité. Le droit africain a place aussi au soleil. Un aparté ? Généralement il ne dure pas aussi longtemps, et se fait sur la scène ! Feraient-il confiance au condamné pour me laisser seul à l'air libre ? J'essaie de faire quelques pas. A ma grande surprise, je suis comme cloué au sol ; comme si des ferrements me retenaient sur place. C'est sans doute, me dis-je, l'effet de la potion de vérité. Ce qui expliquerait cette assurance qu'ils ont de me laisser seul.

Tout d'un coup des cris et des roulements de tam-tams s'arrachèrent à l'horizon, combinés avec de la musique moderne. Je compris ! Ils fêtaient ! Ils fêtaient la victoire et les chefs des délégations. Ils s'y étaient précipités sans plus penser à leur victime. De telles fêtes durent généralement plusieurs jours. Dans l'ivresse générale allaient-ils se souvenir encore de moi ? J'affrontais déjà les murs de l'ostracisme avant même que les délégations aient quitté le couvent du procès ! J'étais relégué dans « l'Archipel du Goulag » de l'oubli.[90] Les eaux du Léthé m'entraînaient vers des rivages infinis ; dans un gouffre sans nom. J'y voyais l'immense armée des humains innocents se précipiter, transportés par des vagues furieuses pour y être dévorés par des monstres marins. Les dieux divorcés avec les humains assistaient stupides à ce spectacle. « Ils riaient entre eux, ils raillaient, ils ricanaient. » Leurs rires sardoniques provoquaient des éternuements mortels. Nous riboulions des yeux, des quinquets. Quoi ? pitié ? Elle avait fui, remplacée par le « passeport jaune ».[91] Débordement des haines assassines assouvies. Flux et reflux de la marée des vivants morts. Ce voyage vers l'oubli des insectes amène, le temps d 'un cillement d'yeux, des millions et des millions d'hommes. Aucune solidarité ne peut en venir à bout. Fatalité dont nous sommes les artisans quotidiens. Tous les jours, pourchassés, réprimés, embarqués, déportés, relégués par des désirs mâles qui

---

90. Referring to *The Gulag Archipelago* (1973), Aleksandr Solzhenitsyn's history of the network of Soviet forced labor camps where many dissidents were imprisoned.

91. An identity card that former convicts had to carry in nineteenth-century France.

en reçoivent quelque prime de plaisir. Comment sauver ces flots successifs que l'oubli entraîne derrière lui dans l'Archipel du Goulag ? Les humains terminent leur course invariablement. La semence de l'oubli se trouve incrustée dans la chair. Elle ronge de nuit, de jour, tel un cancer. La marée humaine, condamnée par cette fatalité, n'a d'autre issue que cette lutte inégale contre les monstres du néant. Niaiseux, englouti déjà dans l'abîme, me tend sans doute la main ! En cet instant je suis peutêtre le seul à le ramener à l'existence ! Il revit. Les êtres humains ne peuvent-ils pas surmonter cette discontinuité qui les fait tour à tour néant, existence ? Chacun de nous est Lazare. Christ.[92]

J'avais perdu de vue un moment la musique et le roulement des tam-tams. Mes yeux ouverts ne voyaient rien autour de moi. J'étais en voyage intérieur. Retranché en moi-même, je contemplais des monstres, des bulles d'air, des lucioles ; des étoiles filantes. J'oubliais, tapi sous mes rêves, le monde des humains. Ils m'ont empêché d'écrire le livre qui aurait constitué la révolution copernicienne du roman. Mais celui de la parole intérieure que j'écris depuis mon arrestation, hors de leur prise et de leur pouvoir, délié de tout appareil de gestes enchaînés, au seuil de l'aurore de l'extériorisation, ils ne peuvent le soumettre à

92. Both the dead man brought back to life and his savior (John 11).

la contrainte de la censure. Il s'élabore libre, tiré de notre fond, établi dans sa réalité, à l'abri du public, assez puissant pour permettre d'extraire de mes moments intimes et de mes fantasmes l'image de mon public, ce parent intérieur indispensable à notre survie d'artiste. Écriture, tu es traîtresse ! Tu te déploies dans la prostitution du corps. Union sadique. Tu accroches la parole comme une proie facile. Elle s'abandonne, telle une fille de la rue. Tu la pourchasses tel le mâle la femelle qu'il convoite, saisit et pénètre. Prostituée, tu t'abandonnnes à toutes les idéologies. Dès l'aurore de l'humanité, celle de la classe dominante vint te flirter. Tu lui enfantas un fils : esclavage. Tu as toujours été du côté des sales bourgeois.

La danse avait redoublé d'intensité et venait trouer ma surdité. Autour de moi, toujours pas d'âme. J'étais peut-être surveillé par un œil invisible. Qui me dévisageait, déshabillait et rhabillait au rythme du tam-tam. Mais je ne cherchais pas à le savoir. L'épaisseur du silence qui m'enveloppait trahissait celle de ma solitude intérieure, pourtant peuplée de créatures suscitées par mes interminables rêves éveillés.

Tout d'un coup, je vis apparaître devant moi une forme humaine. Fantôme ! Un homme ! m'écriai-je ! Un semblable à moi ! Il y avait l'éternité que je n'en avais plus vu. Un mulâtre par-dessus le marché ! Cheveux ébouriffés. Barbe en dentelles. Je me frottai les yeux. L'homme s'approcha. Mais il semblait se gêner dans sa démarche et cachait quelque chose entre ses jambes. Arrivé à quelques pas de mon trône, il s'arrêta comme pour me dévisager. Il me sourit. Puis d'un pas décidé s'avança lestement vers moi et j'entendis un son aigu de clochette. Je reconnus Niaiseux.

— Niaiseux !

— Giambatista Viko !

Il se jeta à mes genoux. Moi, j'étais toujours cloué.

— Giambatista ! Le sort, la fatalité. Le destin. Tu es à présent Giambatista Viko. Tu n'es plus le maître !

— Qu'as-tu fait depuis notre séparation ?

— L'errance dans la propriété, l'immense propriété du couvent. C'est ma condition. L'être humain m'est devenu un étranger. La compagnie des animaux plus familière que celle des hommes. L'errance, c'est cela ! Loin d'eux. Le tintement que tu viens d'entendre sert à me signaler aux femmes. C'est la seule communion que je partage avec elles. Avec les mâles le mépris, la haine. Je suis un paria. Les frères animaux, les chiens, les chats — ils sont légion dans la propriété — me caressent ; je les caresse. Nous nous comprenons. Personne ne s'occupe d'eux. Comme de moi. Compagnons de l'errance dans la nature, nous vivons. Nous haïssons l'espoir.

— Oui ! L'espoir tue quand tout l'horizon est bouché.

— Nous sommes des cobayes.

— Cobayes de la mort de l'espoir ! Le chevalier du Moyen Age errait en quête d'aventures, de « choses spirituelles ». Nous, nous sommes des Galaad sans Graal. L'humain qui aurait pu constituer la quête la plus merveilleuse est mort. Notre aventure n'est plus que le roman du sacrement du néant.

— Du moins apparaît-il ainsi ! Notre roman ne serait-il pas un sacrement d'initiation à ce retour à la nature, à l'eau claire, au chant des oiseaux, à la brise du soir caressant les feuilles d'arbres, courbant l'herbe verte !

Ah ce retour à la nature que la culture occidentale recherche tant ! Ce serait une manière de leçon ? Nous réconcilier avec l'organique, le corps, la nature ; nous réintégrer dans l'univers dont raison et culture nous avaient séparés !

— Mais pour que la nature renaisse en quelque sorte en nous, est-il nécessaire de tuer l'humain ?

— Oui, ressusciter la bestialité pour que l'homme se redécouvre : retrouve sa vraie figure !

— Qui réside dans l'équilibre entre la raison et la nature.

— Le prix de cette renaissance est le service funèbre de la raison !

Après ce bref dialogue je m'aperçus que Niaiseux avait survécu à lui-même malgré cette immersion dans la nature. Sa lucidité était restée sans faille. Le baptême au contraire, au lieu de l'abrutir, l'avait rendu à luimême. L'absence de dialogue avec l'Autre finit par créer la conscience de régression. Simple illusion ! Mais la vie n'est-elle pas une somme d'illusions !

Works Cited in the Novel and in Notes

Althusser, Louis. "Idéologie et appareils idéologiques d'état (notes pour une recherche)." *Positions (1964–1975)*, Les Éditions Sociales, 1976, pp. 67–125.

Amrouche, Jean. *Journal, 1928–1962*. Éditions Alpha, 2009.

Arsan, Emmanuelle. *Emmanuelle*. Éditions Fixot, 1988.

Bachelard, Gaston. *L'air et les songes: Essai sur l'imagination et du mouvement*. José Corti, 1943.

Bécaud, Gilbert. Lyrics to "Quand il est mort, le poète." *Genius*, 2021, genius.com/Gilbert-becaud-quand-il-est-mort-le-poete-lyrics.

Breton, André. *Second manifeste du surréalisme*. 1930. *Manifestes du surréalisme*, J.-J. Pauvert, 1962, pp. 147–226.

Buffon, Comte de. *Discours sur le style*. Edited by Félix Hémon, 5th ed., Charles Delagrave, 1894. epub.ub.uni-muenchen.de/41202/1/8P.gall.2269.pdf.

Césaire, Aimé. *Cahier d'un retour au pays natal*. Présence Africaine, 1983.

———. *The Complete Poetry of Aimé Césaire: Bilingual Edition*. Translated by A. James Arnold and Clayton Eshleman, Wesleyan UP, 2017.

Desnos, Robert. *Corps et biens*. 1930. Bibliothèque Numérique Romande, 2016. ebooks-bnr.com/ebooks/pdf4/desnos_corps_et_biens.pdf.

Fabian, Johannes. *Time and the Other*. Columbia UP, 2014.

Goethe, Johann Wolfgang von. *Faust*. Translated by Victor Lange, Continuum, 1994.

Hugo, Adèle. *Victor Hugo raconté par Adèle Hugo*. Edited by Evelyn Blewer et al., Plon, 1985.

Lacan, Jacques. *Écrits*. Éditions du Seuil 1966.

Leiris, Michel. *Aurora*. Éditions Gallimard, 1946.

———. *Haut mal*. Éditions Gallimard, 1943.

Lévy-Bruhl, Lucien. *Les carnets*. PU de France, 1998.

Malraux, André. *Les noyers de l'Altenburg*. Éditions Gallimard, 1948.

Marx, Karl. Introduction. *A Contribution to the Critique of Hegel's Philosophy of the Right*. 1844. *Marxist Internet Archive*, 2009, www.marxists.org/archive/marx/works/1843/critique-hpr/intro.htm.

Meadows, Donella H., et al. *The Limits to Growth*. Universe Books, 1972.

Michelet, Jules. Preface. *Histoire de France. Project Gutenberg E-book*, 2015, www.gutenberg.org/files/47969/47969-h/47969-h.htm.

Musil, Robert. *"Tonka" and Other Stories*. Translated by Eithne Wilkins and Ernst Kaiser, Secker and Warburg, 1965.

Ngal, Georges. "Introduction à une lecture d'*Epitomé* de Tchicaya U Tam'si." *Canadian Journal of African Studies*, vol. 9, no. 3, 1975, pp. 523–30.

———. "Le théâtre d'Aimé Césaire: Une dramaturgie de la décolonisation." *Revue des sciences humaines*, vol. 35, 1970, pp. 613–36.

Proust, Marcel. *À l'ombre des jeunes filles en fleurs*. Du côté de chez Swann, À l'ombre des jeunes filles en fleurs, pp. 431–955. *À la recherche du temps perdu*, edited by Pierre Clarac and André Ferré, vol. 1, Éditions Gallimard, 1954.

Revel, Jean-François. *Ni Marx ni Jésus: La nouvelle revolution mondiale est commencée aux États-Unis*. 1970. Rev. ed., J'ai Lu, 1973.

Rimbaud, Arthur. *Œuvres complètes*. Edited by Antoine Adam, Éditions Gallimard, 1972.

Rowell, Margit. *La peinture, le geste, l'action: L'existentialisme en peinture*. Klincksieck, 1972.

Senghor, Léopold Sédar. "Le français, langue de culture." *Esprit*, Nov. 1962, pp. 837–44.

Vigny, Alfred de. *Œuvres complètes*. Edited by Paul Viallaneix, Éditions du Seuil, 1965.